CRITICAL RESPONSE T[...]

Straight Razor
"As technically outrageous and emotionally intense as a madman's shotgun held to the temple of contemporary culture. [Jaffe's 12 stories] succeed terrifically."
—Review of Contemporary Fiction

Othello Blues
"Composed almost wholly of stage directions, quick cuts, and dialogue, Jaffe's novel is an imaginative, witty, and politically prescient retelling of *Othello*."
—Thomas LeClair, Electronic Book Review

Eros Anti-Eros
"Jaffe's fictions are a wonder of deadpan humor, biting wit, and visual beauty. No recent fiction has gripped me with such force and immediacy."
—Marianne Hauser

Madonna and Other Spectacles
"Crackling with rage and black laughter, these fictions wrench themselves out of the grimmest facts: genocide, nuclear devastation, black poverty, corporate murder. [This is] a collection that confronts terror in street language and redoubles its impact."
—Publisher's Weekly

Beasts
"Jaffe's convincing portraits of the dispossessed are moving, insightful glimpses of the human spirit under stress."
—The New York Times Book Review

Dos Indios
"Told with the simplicity of a folk tale, this spiritual journey of a Peruvian flute player is a beautiful and moving story."
—Newsday

SEX FOR THE MILLENNIUM

Extreme Tales

Books by Harold Jaffe

Sex for the Millennium (extreme tales)
Straight Razor (stories; visuals by Norman Conquest)
Othello Blues (novel)
Eros Anti-Eros (fictions)
Madonna and Other Spectacles (fictions)
Beasts (fictions)
Dos Indios (novel)
Mourning Crazy Horse (stories)
Mole's Pity (novel)
The American Experience: A Radical Reader (editor)
Affinities: A Short Story Anthology (editor)

SEX FOR THE MILLENNIUM

Extreme Tales

Harold Jaffe

Normal

Published by Fiction Collective Two with support given by the
English Department Unit for Contemporary Literature of Illinois
State University, and the Illinois Arts Council

Address all inquiries to: Fiction Collective Two, c/o Unit for
Contemporary Literature, Campus Box 4241, Illinois State University, Normal, Illinois 61790-4241

Sex for the Millennium
Harold Jaffe

ISBN: Paper, 1-57366-078-7

Library of Congress Cataloging-in-Publication Data
Jaffe, Harold.
Sex for the millennium : extreme tales / Harold Jaffe. -- 1st ed.
p. cm. -- (Black ice books)
ISBN 1-57366-078-7 (alk. paper)
1. Erotic stories, American. 2. Science Fiction, American.
3. Satire, American. I. Title. II. Series
PS3560.A312S49   1999
813'.54--DC21   98-55134
                                                                CIP

Cover Art & Design: Norman Conquest
Book Design: Martin Riker

Produced and printed in the United States of America
Printed on recycled paper with soy ink

ACKNOWLEDGEMENTS

A number of these "extreme tales" were published in the following journals and anthologies: *The Literary Review*; *two girls review*; *Southern Lights*; *The Southern Anthology*; *ACM*; *Fiction International*; *Alt-X*; *CrossConnect; Shincho* (Japan); *Eureka* (Japan).

I'd like to thank Sydney Brown, Samuel R. Delany, Eurydice, Lance Olsen, Stephen-Paul Martin, Jim Miller, Tom LeClair, Larry McCaffery, and Curt White for reading and commenting on this volume in manuscript.

CONTENTS

One

Two

for Tina & Sumi

ONE

"If you have love enough, then go on, rage, rage out of love."

—Friedrich Hölderlin

NINE-INCH HEELS

Where did we meet? The health club.

She was on the stairmaster in a hot pink leotard and black tights with matching pink socks, looking sexy and a little silly, earphones on her head, cracking her gum, striding like a maenad, dyed-platinum ponytail rhythmically swishing, her firm and fully packed heart-shaped butt sticking way out.

What was she listening to on her Sony Sport Walkperson? The score from *Pulp Fiction.*

Or maybe it was Trader Joe's. She was wearing fuchsia clogs and those faded torn jeans young people wear. And she wasn't all that young. Maybe 34. Browsing through the wine section, bending in that way attractive women do, legs straight, rump high in the air. When she straightened, I saw that she was clasping a bottle of California Cabernet. Good label, too. She was no dummy.

Anyhoo. I displayed my charm.

She tossed her auburn shoulder-length hair and assessed the merchandise.

We converged at the juice bar.

Scratch that. Juice bars suck. This is the Millennium. Coffee rules. Starbucks. Espresso macchiato for me, double cappuccino for her. One of her "very few vices," she confided.

Referring to coffee.

I didn't ask the natural next question. Cappuccino cream mustache on her upper lip, she volunteered.

"One of my other vices is I'm a dominatrix."

"That's not a vice," I offered. "That's a capital gain."

She grinned a toothy grin. Evidently she liked financial jokes. Which was fine with me.

Our eyeballs linked.

She drove a puce Honda Accord and I drove a beige Toyota Corolla. Mine was an older model with a dented left rear bumper but had fewer miles.

Followed her back to her place.

One of those condos near, or in, a shopping mall. Erected day before yesterday, aspiring to look old. And her one-bedroom flat was very cozy. At least by current standards. The walls, painted amethyst, contained five framed photographs of execution scenes: hanging, firing squad, lethal injection, two beheadings. Artfully composed. Also a movie poster: *Saturday Night Fever*, featuring John Travolta before he got fat, obscenely rich, and forfeited his rhythm to embrace Scientology.

"Do you mind," she said, "if I change into something more comfy?"

"You can tell by the way I walk my walk / I'm a woman's man / No time fo' talk."

"I didn't know you can sing," she grinned. "Falsetto too."

"Is that a plus?"

"Most definitely. Help yourself to a drug. I'll be right back."

18

Something yelped. Her dog, a yelping schnauzer. In the miniature kitchen, behind a wooden grate.

She returned in a black latex garter belt, black latex thigh-level boots with scarlet nine-inch heels, and an Israeli commando surplus gas mask. Her coral-red nipple attachments were a good five inches long.

I was standing in front of one of her two framed beheadings, naked (except for my knee socks) and erect as a Nazi salute.

"Did I give you permission to get a hard-on?" she reprimanded through her gas mask.

Delete the preceding three paragraphs.

She returned in her gym outfit: leotards, tights, color coordinated accessories, leather Reeboks. I saw that she carried a torture device. No. It was the Abs Roller Plus, designed to tone up your tum.

She set it up on the carpet.

Turned out she sold the thing on commission and spotted me as a thick-waisted potential consumer.

After recovering my composure, I said, "Should I strip down to my briefs?"

"Your call."

"Would you have guessed I wore briefs? Or boxers?"

"With your mustache and given the car you drive, boxers."

That sounded vaguely like an insult but I couldn't be sure.

"I know," I offered, "a quicker way of tuning my abs."

"What's that?"

"Face-sitting."

"You on me or vice versa?"

"Vice versa."

"How will that improve the flab around your middle?"

"If you sit on my face I won't have a chance to eat, right? I mean usual food."

She laughed licentiously. She was a PoMo woman just like I thought.

"Fork over $120 for the Abs Roller Plus," she said, thrusting out her hand, "and I'll sit on your face."

"120 is kind of steep."

"You come on like a high roller. What are you, a street person?"

I didn't know quite how to take that.

"All right," she said. "Make it an even hundred."

"What do I get for the even hundred?"

"An Abs Roller Plus and my ass on your face."

"A new Abs Roller Plus?"

"Yes, new."

"How many minutes of your ass on my face?"

"How many minutes do you want, slave-turd?"

"23."

"No fuckin' way. I'll give you 12 minutes."

"Make it 19."

"Where do you come up with these numbers?"

"I wear a Rolex digital."

"Rolex, eh? I guess you're not a street person. I'll give you 15 minutes of my fine ass on your filthy slave turd face. Final offer."

"Will you grind down?"

"I'll do what I do and you will hold your tongue."

"If I hold my tongue how will I service you, Mistress?"

She flashed me a razor grin. "Do you want to be my sex slave?"

"Is this a . . . proposal?"

"Whatever."

"I'm at a loss for words."

"Which is preferable to pissing from the mouth. Your usual condition."

So it went, the dialogue between Cher, as she called herself, and me, Skip. My actual name is Seward, one of those unaccountable WASP names imposed on innocent, babbling infants by their self-obsessed parents.

In my case, I was named after my paternal grandfather who made big $$$ manufacturing porcelain toilet bowls and toilet accessories like flushers, tanks and the apparatuses inside tanks. People use the toilet and when they're done they pull, push, tug the flushing mechanism, and when something goes wrong they peer inside the tank and make an adjustment. But they rarely consider the unmoved mover, the soul responsible for their hygienic hiatuses.

I came of age in the carefree state of New Jersey. Everyone called me Skip.

The bottom line is nothing happened. Her fax machine started ringing, which set her schnauzer to yelping and wheezing. It was, she claimed, a "hot" fax. Anyway I'd lost my hots. Shoot, I didn't want to pay for it. I was 39-years-old, 6-1, with a thick blond mustache, pretty well built, and hung okay too, even if I didn't have videogenic abs.

I saw Cher again the next day at Starbucks nursing her double cappuccino in its tall fluted glass, the thick hot cream forming a raunchy mustache on her upper lip.

It had rained earlier. Now the sky was clear with a pervasive smell of ozone.

Cher grinned her ass-reaming grin. "Take a load off, Skip. Have some Starbucks coffee."

"No prob. Mind if I stroke your upper thigh under the table?"

Cher glared at me through narrowed eyes.

"I like your cappuccino mustache," I said.

"What's really on your mind, Skip?"

"Disney videos and velcro restraints. What say we go back to my place, Cher?"

"Where do you live?"

"Behind Trader Joe's. I have a lovely condominium."

"Bachelor pad, you mean?"

"Exactly."

"With a circular waterbed?"

"Uh-huh."

"Mirrors on the ceiling?"

"Fuck yeah."

"And a jacuzzi?"

"Naturally."

"Easy access to the World Wide Web?"

"Real easy."

"She and He plush terry calf-length robes for après sex?"

"Yes."

"White or yellow?"

"Turquoise."

"I had a feeling you'd say that," she said. "I hate turquoise plush terry calf-length She and He robes for après sex."

"What are you trying to say, Cher?"

"That you're a fuckin' loser, Skip. I don't and won't sit on a loser's face."

The longhaired waiter delivered my espresso macchiato. I took a long languorous sip. The longhaired waiter watched appreciatively.

"Actually I was envisioning sitting on your face," I said.

The longhaired waiter looked at me inquisitively.

"I'm talking to my friend Cher," I explained.

He nodded and left.

"That's different," Cher said. "I don't have a problem with that."

So it was back to my place, her puce Honda Accord trailing my beige Toyota Corolla with its dented left rear bumper.

She seemed impressed with my framed execution photos on the wall. And my movie poster of *Raging Bull* featuring DeNiro all beefed up as the quick-tempered, two-fisted Italian kid from the slums who rose to become middleweight champion of the world.

"Cher, do you mind if I change into something more comfy?"

"Skip, you're the top so it's your call."

"I thought the bottom had the advantage."

"Explain."

"The eroticized pain of the bottom is richer, less mediated, than the administered pain of the top."

Cher narrowed her eyes. "Okay. I'll buy that."

"Help yourself to a drug. I'll be back."

I returned wearing black leather chaps, a studded snakeskin pouch with snap-off codpiece, a stainless steel full-body harness, barbwire arm bands, lead-filled gauntlet Harley gloves, and a full-face snout helmet in burnished metal. A canister of silver duct tape hung from a steel loop on my chaps. And I carried a braided black leather cat-o'-nine.

When Cher, naked and sitting cross-legged on my Kashmiri carpet, saw me she suppressed a yawn.

Delete the preceding two paragraphs.

I returned wearing Nike cross-training gear and carrying a fold-up Thigh & Butt Suppressor, designed for women by Nike and accompanied by an interactive video.

Cher was a fine-looking lady—for her age—but like most single professionals she was wholly committed to her job and she was stressed. Hence she tended to eat on the run and under-achieve.

She was about to say something, but I held up my hand to forestall speech. I set up the Nike T&B Suppressor on the carpet and launched into my demo. Long story short: She was impressed enough to fork over 100 big ones. Correction, she paid by credit card, Visa, recently embraced and bitten on the neck by Nike, which allowed her an additional four percent discount.

After working out we hit Starbucks. She ordered a water-processed double-decaf cappuccino with soy milk, and I had a decaf latte with organic oat milk, faux but nutritious and 99 percent fat-free.

What about the one percent fat?

Starbucks contributes that to the fight against heart disease.

VAMPIRE

It's an obsession and it's draining me.

Heck, if you're sucking strange fruit you might as well enjoy it.

I enjoy it when I'm doing it. It's afterwards, when I find blood on the hem of my gown.

What do you have in mind?

Stopping. Cold turkey.

What about those commands from the underworld?

Are they actually commands? Or is it in my head? You don't hear anything.

Well, I don't hear what you hear. If that's what you mean. But I'm not undead either. You're 126 years-old, hon.

128.

Look, if you stop sucking strange fruit, what will you do?

Professionally, you mean?

All right. Professionally.

I saw this Yahoo! Inc. ad. They want women who can sound aristocratic online.

Right up your alley.

I just need to conquer this obsession. What time is it?

8:19. There's a full moon tonight. If we can see it through the smog.

Did you hear that?

What?

That beagle that moved in across the street. Barking.

[pause]

What I heard was baying. Beagles don't bay, hon.

You've said you love me. I'm going to ask you to prove it.

How?

When the obsession kicks in, I want you to bind me to the bed.

That's what you usually do to me.

I want you to undress me.

Love to, but why?

If I'm naked I won't go out. No matter how I feel.

Upper-class vampire protocol, eh?

There's something else. That strange fruit you referred to isn't strange. I said I enjoyed it. I don't. Not really. It's stale, insipid.

I gather you still enter through the jugular? Two incisively elegant pinpricks on the throat?

I enter where I can. Sometimes jugular, sometimes down below.

Ah.

As I said, too much of it is stale, dry, hardened.

I think what you're saying, hon, is: people are ugly and juiceless. You've been around a long time. Is it shittier now than before?

Well, the turn of the last century sucked: Pious robber barons. Industrial miseries. The Thirties sucked: Hitler's charisma. Hamstrung Capital. The Forties sucked: Gulags and crematoria. Worldwide fascism. The Fifties sucked: Rooting out the Reds. Complacency fastened to imbecility. I could go on. But this, now, sucks in a new way, resisting definition. Biting into one of them is like swallowing gas: foul, recirculated.

If things are so fucked over now why do you want to get with the program? Link digits with Yahoo! Inc.?

Probably I exaggerate my potential influence, but I'm an idealist. I've been around a long while. At Yahoo! Inc. I can, perhaps, infiltrate. Make an impact.

What sort of impact?

Who was it that said that the United States has proceeded from barbarism to decadence without the intervening stage of civilization? I would like to be a civilizing influence.

I'm impressed. What happens if it doesn't work? You're dismissed as just another do-gooder vampire?

I've prepared for that possibility. That wooden stake in my closet. . . .

Is that what it is? I thought it was another of your sex toys. I have a feeling who the designated stake-driver is.

Yes. It will satisfy your passive-aggressiveness. And put an end to this svelte, glossy-haired vampire with her intimidatingly sexy contralto voice for all time.

Real time, you mean. You'll still glow and suck in our countless representations of you on TV, the Net and in our collective imagination-diskettes.

Whatever.

[pause]

Am I really passive-aggressive? I thought I was a pussy cat.

Can you please suspend thinking about yourself for one minute? I'm the subject of this discourse. Or am I mistaken?

Sorry about that. You're front and center. It's your fifteen minutes, hon. I'll do exactly as you instruct me. I'll remove your burgundy, silken, floor-length, Coco Chanel gown. Is it Chanel or Yves Saint Laurent?

Chanel.

Harold Jaffe

I'll remove your underthings. Are you wearing underthings?

No.

Um. I'll bind you to the bed. Anything else?

Turn the TV to one of those religious channels.

I get you. Jesus on the cross mediated by televangelists in diamond pinky rings. You're making a warding-off gesture with your burgundy cape. I guess I shouldn't have said the name Jesus.

Silence, scumbag.

[Tenderly]: *You haven't called me scumbag in a while.*

Never mind.

Here comes the moon.

Strip me, bind me. Hurry, fool.

Well, there you are, naked and bound to the custom four-poster kingsize waterbed. What do you think of these restraints? I just bought them.

Where?

Orvis. You like them?

Cowhide and velcro?

Ostrich.

Ahh. I feel it. The moon. **[Intoning]:** In the name of the Goddess Diana and her sharp-toothed daughters online and off. . . .

[long pause]

You tugged at your ostrich and velcro binds. You hissed. You produced sounds from deep in your throat. But you made it, hon. The moon is out of sight. I'm proud of you. You know something else. You looked real sexy with those canines flashing.

I'm too well-bred to show the range of emotions I experienced. Ulysses lashed to his mast hearing the Sirens couldn't have felt a sharper pang. The question is how many more times do I have to do this before the obsession is conquered?

Good question, hon.

All right. Release me.

Harold Jaffe

No way.

What do you mean? Undo these binds.

Not until you answer some questions. Who was better hung: Count Dracula or the Wolf Man?

What? **[pause]** Dracula's was longer, the Wolf Man's was thicker.

Elaborate.

Dracula's was sleek as a stainless steel dildo. Brancusi's bird in flight. The Wolf Man's was a length of hangman's rope, thickly braided with pulsing veins.

Pulsing veins?

Yes. Undo these binds.

What about Dr. Frankenstein?

Frankenstein was underdeveloped. The size of my little finger. Why do you think he created the monster? Now will you release me?

The bride of Frankenstein? With her electrified hair.

Oh. She was wet. Always wet. She'd fornicate her

brains out with the monster. Then when he was spent and snoring, she'd turn to the Wolf Man. She loved his thickly-corded penis. All that blood pulsing. Please release me.

Not just yet. You and your canines are naked and bound to the four-poster. Describing those monster genitals has got me hot and bothered. You remember what fellatio means? Blow-job in plain English. I've done you a bunch but I've never been able to get you to do me. Now you have no choice. I want you to open your aristocratic mouth. Wide, like you're at the dentist. Make sure to suck but not bite. You bite and I become undead like you. I don't want to hang around this fucked-over planet. I just want to spray some jizz on your fine-boned face. You bite me, hon, and you stay bound in Orvis-brand ostrich leather and velcro forever. I'm talking real time.

CANCER IS THE MOTHER

Said I had liver cancer. In "a fairly advanced state," he added smugly, then offered me a Marlboro. I slapped him hard across his face and slammed the door.

Stopped at a bar on the corner called The Broke Spoke ordered a double Jack Daniels, took out my small notebook, and composed a wish-list:

—3 sex partners in one whack (*ménage-à-quatre*)
—opium
—exotic travel
—truffles
—ethical murder

The question was: in what order? That took some consideration. I sipped my Jack.

Logically: travel (to Bangkok, say, or Amsterdam or Rio), then truffles, reputedly aphrodisiacal, followed by the ménage, followed by opium, said to be great but not for sex. Then, close to the end, ethical murder.

But murder who exactly?

"Exactly" wasn't the point. Virtually any mid-, or better, high-level technocrat would do. By technocrat, I meant an institutional big who routinely fucked over ordinary people. These bigs aren't hard to find, and they topple like bowling pins.

Despite not having any symptoms I could pinpoint, the doc predicted three to six months. I sipped my Jack, easy going down, no impediment / no pain. Moreover, fantasizing about the wish-list had produced a woody; I felt it pulsing in my jocks.

Do cancer victims get hard-ons?

Money? I possessed eleven credit cards. Easily good for half-a-dozen ass-kicking months. Hell, I was good for half-a-dozen years. Then, if I'm still sexy, file a Chapter 11, start all over.

Finished the Jack, resisted the temptation to have another, waited for my erection to subside, paid and left.

Since I was just two blocks east of Madison Avenue, I stopped into Ralph Lauren and outfitted myself in the casual British-American elegance that conformed to my platonic version of myself. $4300 and worth it.

I hailed a cab and gave my address, but halfway down Fifth felt that woody starting to swell. I redirected the cabbie to a massage parlor on 40th and Lex. Called Siam, I'd passed it many times and wondered, but never stopped in until now.

The plump, thirtyish Asian female in a geisha outfit bowed me welcome, led me to a small perfumed room, asked how long I meant to stay, took my credit card and instructed me to undress and lie on the rack.

She returned a few minutes later, had me sign for the credit, then left again. Oddly, I wasn't in a hurry, lying on my back in the warm fragrant room, semi-hard penis curling up around my navel. When she returned she closed and locked the door and told me to turn on my stomach.

In response to my question, she said her name was

Keiko. After a perfunctory kneading, she had me turn over and commenced with the real deal. I asked how much it would cost for a second masseuse. She paused and looked at me inquisitively. She said it would cost double the price, but that the other "girl" was engaged with another client.

I motioned her to continue. She certainly knew what she was doing. Or maybe it was my peculiar sensitivity.

Cancer-induced.

Imagining the C-word—incapacitating, deathly, sex-less in the extreme—my erection buckled. I willed myself to recover.

I asked Keiko whether she would undress. She quoted a price, I paid in cash, she undressed. On my back I stroked and squeezed her plump, firm body with one hand while she kneaded my sex with two. Yes, I'm rather large. But then her hands were small. She was, she said (in response to my question), part Korean, part Puerto Rican.

I ejaculated pridefully. Three gushy spurts, three medium, and three juniors. All threes, maybe that signified something. Even Keiko's impassive face seemed impressed.

Back at my condo, feeling a slight post-orgasmic depression, I ignored the three messages on the machine and pulled out some travel books and atlases. Deciding, finally, that I would travel to all three: Amsterdam, Bangkok, and (if I still had my chops) Rio.

After Rio I would return to this benighted country and murder me three technocrats. Unless, of course, I ran into murderable techs on the road.

I flew to Amsterdam three days later and checked

43

into the Grand Hotel Krasnapolsky, just west of the Red Light district. Had a few Dutch gins then lay down on the queen-sized four-poster to sleep off the jet lag. I awoke at three a.m., fully awake, showered, slipped into my Ralph Lauren wide-wale cords, plush Lauren turtle, Lauren tweed hacking jacket, and went downstairs to the cafe. It was the weekend and it was A'dam, so there were souls—tourists and locals—drinking, hanging out.

Ordered a rum and espresso.

Nursing my rum, fantasizing, I smelled a delicate floral scent and looked up to see a raven-haired woman sitting across from me at the small table. She seemed to be appraising me ironically with just the trace of a smile on her handsome, mobile, full-lipped mouth.

"You could get hurt," she said. "You could get sick. You could do all these things, and if you don't have intimate relationships that are strong, you're really alone. But alone is something I know how to do. Intimacy comes and goes. Alone is forever. Be single. Be plural. Just be."

Actually she didn't say that. I spoke first.

"Sorry," I murmured. "I didn't see you."

"What are you sorry about?" she said softly. Smooth mezzo, ambiguously accented.

"Brevity, banality, barbarity."

She laughed full-throatedly. I liked that.

"Can I buy you a drink?" I said.

"What are you drinking?"

"Dark rum and espresso."

"The same."

Cancer Is the Mother

I flagged the waiter then turned back to her. Graceful carriage, supple shoulders, glossy black hair pulled back away from her wide forehead into a plaited chignon. (Did her hair reach the small of her back? Could she sit on it?) Delicate ears with rather large silver hoop earrings. Nationality? Eurasian, Moroccan. . . .

"You are trying," she said, " to place me."

I nodded.

"My name is Dido."

"Ah."

"So you've come to Amsterdam to. . . ."

Sipping my rum, gazing into her clear, deep black eyes.

"Fuck and suck three beautiful females," I blurted. *"En ménage."*

"Must they be beautiful?"

"No. Appealing would do."

"Must they be precisely female?"

"Well. . . ."

"I believe I can help you," Dido said, eyes shining.

She suggested I meet her at Oudekerk in the Red Light area at 3 p.m. Then she stood, smoothing her magenta skirt over her hips. Full hips, muscular long legs. Smiling faintly, she pivoted and left. Her elastic, sensual, yet oddly frail walk reminded me of Buñuel's appreciative comment about Jeanne Moreau's walk during the filming of *Diary of a Chambermaid.*

Before I knew quite what I was doing, I dropped onto my knees and pressed my face against the seat where she had sat. Still warm, smelling faintly of scent.

45

Just then, my face on her vacated seat, but at the same time scanning the high-ceilinged room, I saw Dido at the other end of the cafe turn and nod her head slowly, perhaps smiling.

Back in my room at 4:33 a.m., I was suddenly tired, despite the caffeine.

I slept and dreamt.

When I awoke it was nine a.m., someone tapping at my door.

I cleared my throat.

"Come in."

The door handle turned and a gaunt woman in white entered carrying a staff. Death come to fetch me. No. It was the chambermaid with a mop. She resembled my mother whom I'd just been dreaming of. She promised to come back.

I showered, shaved, slipped on some Lauren a.m. wear and went downstairs. Truffle-shopping time. I asked the soul at the desk, who seemed to ponder. Motioned me to wait and went through a door; when she returned she gave me a small map with a penciled cross southwest of center.

I'm generally a poor navigator, but the map was easy to follow; it led me into the Red Light area, but not to a greengrocer, as I expected. To a restaurant that specialized in truffles and other fungi. It was closed, but would re-open at seven p.m.

Though it was a few minutes after ten, some of the prostitutes in their glass cages were up, displaying themselves. There were clients. I watched a tall, rigid man with a grey brush-cut who looked like a Danish Calvinist minister go into the windowed cubicle of a dominatrix done up in black latex from head to boot. She wore a black gas mask which resembled a pig's snout.

Coincidentally, on the way back to the hotel, I noticed a "specialty" shop on Warmoestraat. Stopped in there and did something I'd always thought of doing: outfitted myself in black latex. Sans gas mask.

Freshly showered and scented (does liver cancer smell?), wearing a Lauren ensemble of *cafe au lait* suede bucks, hacking jacket, indigo denim shirt and camel cords (black latex briefs underneath), I was standing outside the cavernous chapel of Oudekerk, the oldest church in A'dam, dating from the early 14th century, in the very groin of the Red Light area.

Three minutes past three when I watched Dido turn the corner and approach, in purple velvet slacks and yellow clogs, clop-clop on the cobblestones, regal carriage, sexy-frail Jeanne Moreau walk.

She offered her strong slender hand.

We walked south along OZ Voorburgwal hearing the mallards make their kwek/kwek, yeeb/yeeb in the ancient canals, then east at Bloedstraat into a narrow, intricately gabled wooden building, up three flights of dank dark stairs into a flat with muted light. The hostess was a stout middle-aged apparent female, her dyed black hair puffed out into a faintly absurd bouffant, white makeup mask accented with a bloody gash of lipstick.

We sat on a deep sofa in the small parlor sipping

Genever, contemplating the odd-looking canapés on a silver filigreed tray.

"Truffles," Dido anticipated my question.

I tried one. Tasted like a cross between a mushroom and a cocktail onion. Popped a few more.

Then up the winding stair leading to a wide, low-ceilinged bedroom, the fading light slanting through bamboo shades.

The square-shaped bed was low to the floor. The floor was wide-planked hardwood, painted white. Fringed, vari-colored rugs on the floor.

On top of a small wood table were the oils and scents. The space smelled faintly of frangipani.

A woman appeared, young and slender, Thai, or Indonesian, downcast gaze. Barefoot, wearing a silver and green silk robe, loosely tied.

Then another, black, full-figured in her jade green mini and pale yellow halter, perhaps Caribbean, with a beguiling kitten's face and long, intricate dreads.

And then (mild surprise) Dido, my guide, naked, pneumatic, with nipples that stuck out like miniature candied apples. Un-plaited, her glossy black hair reached the small of her back.

The lust was multiform, variegated, but deliberately paced somehow, as though video'd then replayed at a slower speed. I was led through graded depths, artifice. Twist, torque, extend, extend. Moans without sound.

What about the truffles? Were they aphrodisiacal?

Yes, they were. Or maybe it was Frau Death, lingering.

I will remember the smells. Interface of imposed fragrance, frangipani in particular, with the natural smells of the lusting bodies.

As to whether the females were precisely female, in Dido's words. I think they were, but can't absolutely vouch for the slender Asian with her articulate feet. Her feet were pointed, delicate, but also supple, almost prehensile. Much of her sexual energy was generated from the waist down.

She seemed impressed with my latex briefs.

Gratifying.

I felt purged though not shriven.

Back at last in the Grand Hotel Krasnapolsky, I slept the sleep of the just.

Jump-start cancer victim eluding the Big D.

I awoke abruptly at three a.m. with a word on my lips: "More."

Which could only mean opium.

That epiphany birthed this one: Why not commit ethical murder, then smoke opium? That way I'd have something pleasurable to fantasize about.

On that gracious note I fell into sleep.

Awake again at 7:30, I slipped on my Lauren calf-length, turquoise terry robe and picked up the *International Herald Tribune* left outside the door.

Ha. An American "trade delegation" with ties both to the US government and to Microsoft would be in Amsterdam to confer with EU reps. A presentation by a Microsoft VP named F. Jared Baldwin was scheduled at the new trade center just north of the city at noon.

Harold Jaffe

As planned, I met Dido at breakfast (croissants, *cafe au lait*). She wore shiny silver pants and a maroon sweater with a Maltese cross on a silver chain about her slender neck. Her hair was freshly washed, pulled up, fragrant. Her black eyes glowed. She said:

"A former car salesman who for three years pretended to be dying of cancer—even shaving his head and faking seizures—was awarded 13 months in prison. The perpetrator, 50, was also ordered to repay nearly $43,000 to his victims and perform 300 hours of community service. The perpetrator claimed to have kidney, lung and prostate cancer. His former wife and three stepsons believed him, as did most of his fellow residents. To convince people, the perpetrator shaved his head, talked about how awful chemotherapy was and dropped red dye in his toilet to make it look like there was blood in his urine. He also faked seizures, sometimes slamming his head into walls to make the episodes look realistic."

Actually Dido didn't say all that. I spoke first.

"I want to commit ethical murder."

She said: "What will you wear?"

"'DeathLust & Leisure,' by Ralph Lauren. Brushed taupe canvas trousers, mocha suede vest, Norfolk herringbone tweed jacket in olive with navy blue leather accents, modified riding-to-hounds boots, Royall Lyme all-purpose lotion."

Long pause.

"Go for it," Dido said at last.

She waited in the lobby while I went upstairs to change.

50

She led me to a small shop in a mews off Nieuwmarkt where I purchased a Beretta 9mm semi-automatic mini with a fitted silencer.

Time on our hands, Dido and I walked to the Asian sector of the Red Light district near Zeedijk. I told her I was contemplating an opium smoke after the murder, and Dido confirmed that there were opium cellars in the area, pointing to one beneath a cafe called Mexico City.

F. Jared Baldwin, the Microsoft VP, was out of Central Casting: late forties, square-jawed, pulsing cheekbones, gleaming teeth, ears close to the head, gray-blond hair like a carefully mowed lawn, shiny black tasseled shoes.

The Dutch aren't security conscious (unless they're colonizing Africans). I got close enough to Baldwin to smell his cologne. Popped him as he was milling about after his presentation. A single silent round in his tanned neck beneath his custom haircut. No biggie. Dido and I were out of the building by the time Baldwin's handlers and their swinging nametags saw that they had dead doo.

The opium (in the cellar of Cafe Mexico City, on Zeedijk) was as advertised. Dido showed me how to address the pipe, inhale just so, how long to keep it down. My unzippered mind moved, skittered, sidled to the smooth assassination of Baldwin, replaying it with a difference, in, out, around, that sad-happy song, infinitely displayed, figured, filigreed, unfucked over. I also sang along with cancer, the Big C, and that was fruity too. In its way it was as good as the *ménage-à-quatre*. Well, almost. I'm a sex guy, always was. My poppy head in Dido's fragrant lap.

Harold Jaffe

At breakfast the next morning, croissants, kippers, *cafe au lait*, I asked Dido whether she would accompany me to Bangkok. She said:

"A toddler with a rare condition that makes her face hairy like a werewolf's began a series of surgical procedures aimed at improving her appearance and, more importantly, keeping her safe from cancer. The three-year-old child faced a life of isolation, as well as the possibility of an early death from her condition known as congenital hairy nevus but also characterized as 'human werewolf syndrome.' According to her doctor, the surgery, if successful, 'could improve her appearance 300%, but cancer was, and always would be, waiting for her to make a single wrong move.'"

That, I knew, was Dido's way of saying "yes."

Three days later we were in that dusky jewel of the East: Bangkok.

212
MOTHERFUCKERS

My name is Flabass. I'm a shockjock.

So this dude with a thick Bronx accent phones the station and says: I seen that you had porn star Amber Viper on right before she broke her own world record of doing 212 guys. Well, I was one of 'em. Number 192 to be exact. How's about I come on your show, give you the skinny?

I'm like: You were one of the 212 motherfuckers that got it on with Amber Viper?

Uh-huh.

You sound kind of dense. Know how to get to Manhattan from the Bronx?

I may be dense but I ain't dumb.

So he comes on the program looking like you'd expect: Chunky, balding, working-class, a little dense and a little dumb.

You know who I am?

Sure. Flabass, the world-famous shockjock.

Ever been on TV before?

Nope.

Nervous?

Nah. Maybe a little.

What do they call you?

Dominic. Dom.

You're Italian, right?

Hundred percent.

You hung pretty good? Italian guys are usually hung.

Yeah, I'm cool.

You don't look that cool. You're sort of a homely dude, right?

That depends.

Depends on if you're blind or not. Let's say you're not handsome. Can you live with that?

Uh-huh.

So how did a homely—check that: unhandsome—guy become part of the 212 motherfuckers that did Amber Viper?

I seen the ad and auditioned.

What'd you have to do? Drop your drawers?

Yeah. And bring proof you're HIV-free.

[Laughs] That's real hard to scam, right?

Plus you had to wear a rubber.

Bring your own?

Nah. They had like a huge crate filled to the brim with rubbers. And another crate for the used ones.

It was in Madison Square Garden, right?

Yeah. The Garden.

So how'd they decide the order, like who went first, who went last?

They gave us numbers when we came in. The first, like, ten slots or so were reserved for pros, porn stars.

Amber got a jump-start with the porn stars then took on the ordinary dudes?

Right.

Where? Like on a kingsized circular waterbed or something?

Kingsized but not a waterbed. Probably they were afraid it would burst. All that fucking. The bed was on a thick rug with lots of cushions. There was also kind of a long velvet sofa. And a swing, or sling.

So there was variety, right?

Yeah.

The deal was she had to do one dick at a time, right? No multiples.

Yeah. One at a time.

You were, what? 196th? How long did that take?

I was 192nd. Took about eight hours.

Long time. Were you stripped or dressed?

I stripped down about forty-five minutes before. Other guys kept dressed to the last minute.

You stayed there the whole time? Madison Square Garden?

No. I got something to eat with a bunch of other guys who were at the end of the line like me.

[Laughs] What'd you eat? Raw oysters?

Nah. Fastfood stuff. Burgers.

So you finally got your chance of a lifetime: the 196th guy to fuck Amber Viper. There was no foreplay, right?

No. In and out, shoot your wad. Well, the porn stars, the first like ten guys or so, they messed around with her a little. But not us ordinary guys.

Messed around meaning. . . .

Squeezed her plants. Sucked them. Head.

Harold Jaffe

Went down on her?

Both ways. She did them too.

But one at a time, right? No multiples.

One at a time.

So how did you stay hot all that time?

They had dancing girls, strippers, doing some shit while Amber was being fucked.

Doing some shit? Not touching you?

No. Just stripping, spreading. Like that.

Pretty hot?

Yeah. Not bad.

How about the porn stars that did Amber first? Well-hung, good-looking studs, right?

Yeah. Smooth operators. Not like us ordinary guys.

You should've brought your cellphone. Broadcast the action.

Wasn't allowed. No cameras, camcorders, cellphones, none of that.

So Amber went for eight hours without taking a break, or what?

She took a couple breaks. Fifteen, twenty minutes. Took a leak or something.

She seem to be enjoying it?

Sort of. Hard to say. She wanted to break her record, right? Every time another guy spritzed, the number flashed on a scoreboard.

Probably the same scoreboard the Knicks use.

Right. I think it was.

So what kind of sounds did they have? Piped-in music?

Yeah. Heavy metal. Real loud.

To keep the energy level up, right? Particularly after the first 180 or so.

Yeah.

How'd the place smell? Raunchy?

They had a couple guys with large mops cleaning up after every five or six dudes. It smelled like a locker room.

So finally your turn came, right? Dominic from the Bronx. Were you stiff? Were you ready to rumble?

Shit yeah.

You do it on the bed or the swing?

Bed. She only used the swing with the first ten guys, the porn stars.

How'd you do it? Front? Back?

Back. Some guys she was on her front, some on her side. Me, she got on all fours.

[Laughs] In your case Amber didn't want to see who she was fucking.

[Laughs] Yeah.

So was she tight? **[Laughs]**

She's a small woman, right? Amber. No, she wasn't that tight. I got my eight or ten thrusts then I spritzed.

Way to go, Dominic. She say anything to you?

No, not really.

She moan?

Nah.

Maybe she didn't know you were inside her.

She knew.

Right. You're Italian and you're hung. Okay. So you

pulled out, shook off the used condom, dropped it into the crate filled with used condoms. What'd you do then?

Got dressed and went home.

You didn't even have a cold one? To celebrate?

Nah.

So you took the subway up to the Bronx?

Right.

You didn't get mugged on the subway, did you?

Got hassled but not mugged. No big deal.

Who hassled you?

Nazi skinheads. They must've smelled the sex on me. Got them all worked up. I showed them what I was carrying and they backed off.

Which was?

Smith .357.

That's illegal, Dominic.

So's spitting in the subway. Which I do all the time.

So did you see your girlfriend that same night?

Yeah. I seen her.

Did she know you did Amber Viper? That you were one of the 212 motherfuckers? Number 196?

192. No way. I didn't tell her squat.

What's her name? Your girlfriend?

Regina. Gina.

Sounds like she's Italian too.

Hundred percent.

So did you have enough left to fuck Gina that night?

Shit yeah. Did her from behind. Great action. Probably the best ever.

And all the time you were thinking of Amber Viper, right?

Nah. Well, maybe a little bit.

What'd you do after you did Gina from behind? Have a spaghetti dinner?

Linguine.

The next day Amber Viper phones the station and I take the call.

Flabass, that guy you had on the show yesterday that claimed he did me?

Dominic from the Bronx. Number 196 of the 212 motherfuckers.

He's full of shit. I never saw him before.

What? How would you know? I mean 212—

I remember the face and anatomy of every dude I fucked. That loser wasn't one of them. Trust me.

[pause]

That fuckin' scumbag, I say. He scammed me.

He scammed you and he libeled me. I fucked 212 motherfuckers, which is a new world record, breaking my old record of 200, set last year in the Rose Bowl. Like some girls, they do big numbers but with multiples, okay? I did 212 dudes in Madison Square Garden, one-by-one, and each and every one had class. This bozo that came on your show and claimed he did me—

Dominic from the Bronx.

Yeah. Totally classless.

Yeah, right. Only he got himself some bigtime air-time. At my expense. He outfoxed Flabass. The fuck.

CODY IN JUNE

That night you been asking about was an accident. I just put the pillow over her head to shut her up, not to kill her.

Why shut her up? What was she doing?

She was squealing. I couldn't stand the sound. I told her to shut up.

She didn't like what you were doing to her?

No, she did like it. I told you we been having an affair for a long time.

How long?

Ten years, twelve. It started after I got out of Folsom. But we'd been doing some stuff even before then.

What do you mean: "some stuff"? Intercourse?

No. Not really. Messin' around. Like what she done to me when I was a kid.

At what age did she start molesting you?

Harold Jaffe

Far back as I remember. Me and my brother both.

The brother that's in Quentin, right? Charley?

Chucky. That's what we called him.

Did Chucky ever have intercourse with her?

I don't know. Don't think so. He's been doin' time since he was, like, nineteen. Before that he wasn't around that much.

So you started having intercourse with your mother ten or twelve years ago. Did you ever have any trouble performing?

Like . . . what do you mean?

Not being able to stay hard? Coming too soon?

Nah. Well, it was harder when we, like, begun. I mean, begun screwing. Then it got easier.

She liked it?

Better than me. That's why she would squeal like that. She knew I didn't like that sound. I told her.

Was your mom the only person you were having intercourse with?

I went to hookers now and then.

You enjoyed that?

Yeah. It was all right. I don't like paying for it.

What about in prison?

What do you mean?

You were raped in prison, weren't you?

When I first got sent up. I was a kid, right? 160 pounds. They copped me like they cop pretty much every kid. Right then's when I started pumping iron, building myself up. The next year I was up to 215. So that was the end of them copping me.

Did you cop anyone yourself, Cody?

I done my share, I guess. That's the way it is. Dudes I punked, for the most part they wanted it. I mean they was queer.

You said your mother liked having intercourse with you more than you did, right?

Right. Uh-huh.

Harold Jaffe

If you didn't like it that much why didn't you just stop?

I don't know. I was thinking of stopping. We were doing it, like, twice a week, but then I backed off, kept away for almost a month. She didn't like that. She kept phoning me.

You were living at the shelter then?

When?

When she was phoning you. When you killed her.

Right. Uh-huh.

So she was phoning you at the shelter?

Phoning, sometimes coming down there. She didn't like to come down there, but she did.

She didn't like you living at the shelter?

No. She wanted me to live with her. In her place.

Her studio apartment on. . . .

Tokyo.

Would've been pretty close quarters: you and your mom in that studio apartment on Tokyo Street.

Yeah.

You're a big dude and she was about as large as you. Maybe even larger.

She was pretty large.

But that cramped studio apartment on Tokyo Street is where she was living for a long time and where you had intercourse with her on the average of twice a week for ten or twelve years, right?

Right. Uh-huh.

And that's where you killed her. What were you doing the night of the killing?

Like I said, I was driving around with my buddy. Kyle.

In the stolen Nissan Maxima?

Right.

You'd been drinking?

We was drinking Mexican beer and Geritol.

Geritol because it. . . .

It's a rush. Kind of stimulates you.

So you got stimulated and drunk both?

Not really drunk. Well, pretty close, I guess.

Then what happened, Cody? Describe it in your own words.

I already did.

Do it again. This is a different sector.

Kyle and me got pretty fucked up, I guess, and I sort of told him that I was fucking her. My mom. He said he'd like to watch me do it. So I phoned her. I didn't say anything about coming over with Kyle. And when she saw him she didn't like it. Sort of started screaming at me. But when I made like I was going to leave, she settled down. She gave Kyle a cold beer from the fridge and he sat down on the kitchen chair. Me and her got undressed and laid down on the bed. When I stuck it inside her she started the squealing which she knew I hated. It was even louder than usual. Maybe because Kyle was watching. I think maybe she was getting into it. Kyle being there and all. It was, like, turning her on. Only it wasn't doing that much for me. I just wanted to get it over with, and when she started squealing I guess I sort of lost it.

You talk about sticking it in. There wasn't any fore-play?

You mean. . . .

Sucking and tonguing each other. That sort of thing.

When we started, like the first couple years, she used to, like, suck me. But then it became just the actual screwing.

So did Kyle like what he was watching?

He never said. He just sort of sat there suckin' his beer. I think once he got up and got another Bud from the fridge. I think they found two empty bottles there. The police.

Whose idea was it to cut the body up?

Kyle. Like I said to those others. After I killed her he got real nervous. He was afraid he'd be held as an acces-sory or something. Which'd make his third strike. Which'd mean life and no parole. So he came up with the idea of slicing her. He got the knives and stuff.

From where?

He had 'em. He had all kinds of weapons and shit. He left and came back with a cleaver, saw and some other heavy duty blades in a duffel bag. He also brought a bunch of those garbage bags.

How long was he gone?

I don't know. Hour?

What were you doing alone with your dead mother on the bed in the cramped room?

Nothing. Just sitting against the wall smoking.

Did you think maybe Kyle wouldn't come back? That maybe he'd turn you in?

I didn't think one way or the other. I didn't care. I knew it was the end of the line.

If you knew it was the end of the line why did you cut up your mother's body?

Kyle did most of the cutting. I just sort of went along with it.

What would've happened if you had told him: No, you didn't want to cut up her body? Were you scared to tell him that?

No, I wasn't scared.

Cody in June

[pause]

At what point did you and Kyle have sex?

After we cut it up and put it in the garbage bags.

How many garbage bags did it take?

I don't know. A lot.

Must've been a messy job. Large as she was.

Yeah.

Yet with your mother's blood all over your bodies and on the walls and ceiling, and the whole place stinking of your mother's blood and body parts, you and Kyle had sex. Your mom's blood and stuff turned you on, right?

Not me. Kyle sort of got turned on, I guess. I went along with it.

Was it good sex? Did you enjoy it?

I don't know.

You sodomized him didn't you?

You mean. . . .

Harold Jaffe

You fucked Kyle in the ass?

Yeah.

In the same bed where you did your mom?

Well. . . . Yeah.

And you both came? Ejaculated?

I guess so. Yeah.

[pause]

So, Cody, are you sorry for what you did to your mother? Her name was June, right? Your mom?

Yeah. June. Sure I'm sorry. I'm real sorry.

14 WAYS OF LOOKING AT A SERIAL KILLER

i

10:52 a.m. Two customers were in the adult video shop called Leather & Lace: the serial killer and Gen-X female.

The fem had been spending a long time browsing in the bondage section, leafing through mags, ogling the pix on the video boxes, handling the sex toys.

Sean sidled up to her as she was squatting, fingering the wood grain of a paddle, and said in his soft, deceptive Mickey Rourke voice: "You into whuppin' ass or gettin' your own ass whupped?"

Glaring up at him, the fem was like: "Wha?" Then, recovering, standing tall, she said: "None of your goddamn business."

Sean shrugged, gave his crooked grin, ambled away, saying real soft over his shoulder, "Just wonderin'."

Whereupon the fem shouted harshly: "That's your problem, asshole."

According to Burt Denny, 47, the porno clerk on duty who observed the exchange, Sean the serial killer "nodded his head real slow without turning around."

"Lucky she wasn't a redhead," Denny explained to investigators. "Or she'd be spitting teeth."

ii

Police in Kingman, AZ—where Sean had friends in an area trailer park—were looking at Sean in connection with the 1997 disappearance of Betti-Jean Haffner, a would-be supermodel who disappeared one day after a trip to a laundromat.

A police spokesperson said that Haffner was a self-confessed "phoneaholic" who made as many as 525 calls a week, the majority on her cellular phone. Police became suspicious when the calls abruptly stopped.

Haffner was an athletic redhead with cropped hair. The six California women Sean is charged with slaying also had red cropped hair and were very fit.

Betti-Jean Haffner's remains were never found.

iii

As a cost-saving measure, Los Angeles County officials voted unanimously to shut down all public inpatient and outpatient facilities for the mentally ill, effective October 1.

The *Times* reports that law enforcement is bracing for waves of the mentally ill to hit the streets. But experts warn that many more police will be needed to defuse potentially volatile situations involving mentally ill people lacking treatment and medication.

As one top cop, requesting anonymity, put it: "If you move the cops into position to take on mad-dog terror attacks from the mentally ill, you're leaving the inner cities with at best a minimal police presence. Which would almost certainly result in unprecedented crack-induced violence, arson and plunder."

"What about mobilizing the National Guard?"

"You're yanking my bone! National Guard's a bunch of weekend wusses. The psychos would run roughshod over them."

iv

Several neighbors described Sean as a loner. One, Les Deal, said Sean, who lived in a Contra Costa condo, came and went "like a ghost at odd hours of the night."

Deal said Sean never had a girlfriend and "didn't seem to have great relationships with women."

"There was just something a little bit different about him," Deal added. "Like an anger, or rage, that would come out from time to time. I don't know what was bugging him."

On Nov. 20, the day after Betti-Jean Haffner disappeared, Deal said he was struck by the length of time Sean spent cleaning his Mazda Miata in the front yard.

"Heck, he cleaned that thing every which way but loose," Deal said. "A Miata is a small Oriental car, but he must've spent six hours cleaning it inside and out."

v

The Unabomber is demented.
Well, he killed innocent industrial scientists, didn't he?

79

The Unabomber's assault on the industrial-techno-logical system was generated by his own maladjustment and frustration.

I'm with you on that one.

Moreover he is impotent.

Sexually?

Socially. Like an introvert.

Introverts are dysfunctional dreamers.

Did you read his so-called treatise?

Who?

The Unabomber.

It's on my list, but I haven't gotten to it yet.

It was summarized on CNN. And on the World Wide Web. He gets all worked up by so-called genetic engineering. The same genetic engineers that allegedly want to make everyone talk, think, dream, shit and screw alike will find the cure for cancer.

We hope and prey.

Of course there's a bunch of new diseases—like those flesh-eating viruses, for example—that are liable to nail us. But cut our top scientists enough slack and they'll eradicate this new deal too.

By enough slack you mean dollars?

Dollars. Freedom. Freedom to delete sociopaths like the Unabomber as soon as his funky introversion is uncovered. Psychological profiles I've seen calculate that he was an antisocial, glue-sniffing little asswipe who hated competitive sports.

By delete you mean kill? Or lock him up?

Hell. You lock him up you got to segregate his bony ass, else he jump-starts the brains of demented black cons. Those bloods pump iron and pray to Allah. Once he gets into their skulls the shit hits the collective fan. Lot of those musclebound apes get released from prison.

Not so much anymore with the Three Strikes law.

Three Strikes is hype and bulldick, okay. Problem is with the US judiciary. Getting the bad dudes behind bars in the first place is what's jacking us off. And you know whose fault that is?

You're asking me?

That's right.

Well, Newt and his allies say media. Those card-carrying politically-correct liberals that control the media.

Newt. How much advance did Rupert Murdoch give him for his new non-book?

The figure I heard was four million.

Hey, anyone that can get four mil for thumping his titties and talking out of his flabby butt has got to know his shit, right?

vi

Like most serial murderers in this day and age, Sean is handsome. Maybe handsome is not the right word. Videogenic. That's how he charms those redheads. Chiseled cheekbones, straight blond long hair, designer stubble, small ears close to his head. And that crooked grin with those white, straight teeth. Law enforcement speculates that it's a bridge since being on the road like he is he wouldn't be able to brush and floss regular to keep those choppers healthy white.

He's not that tall, about six feet, but he's wiry strong with broad shoulders, long sinewy arms, real defined abs, and muscular thighs from grippin' his Harley.

The tattoos begin at the back of his neck and motorcross down his body to his ankles. He even has a tat on his penis, the outline of his home state, Texas, with the name "Jody" inside Texas. Jody was one of his early girl-friends who disappeared and whose remains were never found.

She had red cropped hair.

Inside the "o" of Jody there's a tattooed scorpion. Which has puzzled law enforcement.

Inside the upcurved tail of the scorpion is tattooed the word "Mom." Like most serial killers Sean loved his mom who died of colon cancer when he was real young. He hated his stepdad who abused and molested him.

I have a feeling you're wondering how he can have such a complexly interesting tattoo on his penis. He just happens to be hung like a horse. Plus he's uncut.

Which is great to listen to Nine Inch Nails with.

Talkin' 'bout Sean the serial murderer.

vii

Evidently Sean's modus operandi was to scout work-ing-class bars and county fairs for athletic redheads. In at least one instance, Dolores "Pinky" Hanson, Sean persuaded her to get her shoulder-length red hair cropped.

Then he cropped her.

Sean picked up Pinky in a county fair in Needles, California on Friday afternoon, Sept 16, at around 1:15. She got her hair cut at Rhoda's Coifs that same afternoon at 4:45. That evening they checked into Hitch's Motel, 23 miles west of Needles on I-40.

Sean signed his name John Wayne Gacy, which was a grisly private joke, since Gacy was a notorious serial murderer of young boys.

Gacy liked to dress up as a clown to lure young boys. He also drew portraits of himself dressed as a clown which, since his execution, have been selling for top $$ in galleries throughout the country.

Indications are that Sean had sex with Pinky in Hitch's Motel, then strangled her. Or, alternatively, strangled her in the process of having sex, that is, while he was climaxing.

They were doing it from the back, doggy style.

It is likely that Pinky was climaxing as well. Since one of Sean's boasts, after a sixpack or two, was that he had never banged a fem that failed to climax. Not just once but multiple times.

I guess he was never with a female on a SSRI. Serotonin Re-Uptake Inhibitor. Those puppies make women anorgasmic.

But once technology tweaks Viagra to make it work for fems it will counter the sexual depression of SSRI's.

Harold Jaffe

Why should dudes get all the sweets?

Forensic tests turned up Sean's sperm—and plenty of it—in Pinky Hanson.

They know the sperm is Sean's because of DNA.

viii

A money manager and a serial killer were standing side-by-side in a public urinal.

Please don't take this wrong, the money manager said. But you piss like a horse.

I only go once a day. And this is it.

Once a day. Amazing. And you look like a guy that drinks a lot of beer.

I like my brew. I won't deny it. You're not doing all that bad. For a short guy.

I'm just about done. Few more shakes and that's it. Shake, shake / zip 'em up. Sounds like you're just getting rolling. Pleased to meet you. I'm a money manager.

I'll shake your hand when I'm finished. Okay?

No problem. I can see that both your hands and just about all your fingers are engaged. I'll just lean against this funky wall. If it's okay with you. What did you say you did?

I'm a serial killer. Sort of in between jobs.

Just about everybody I know is like that. Out of work or almost out of work. On the bubble. I hate that phrase. This darn recession. I guess I'm one of the lucky ones.

You, lucky? You look like a wuss with short legs. My

guess is you're short all over. But you're good at managing money, right?

That's what I do, okay? And, yes, I'm good at it. Some time—if you're interested—I'll show you my commendations. Well, you're good at pissing. You haven't lost a beat. How many you kill?

How many? Twenty-two. Well, maybe twenty-three. One is still in the hospital. Intensive care.

ix

Male Serial killers are into anal sex. That's been amply documented. But Sean was a little different in that he preferred the front. Clarification: he preferred the front *from the back*, doggy style, like with Pinky. But what he also liked was the fem to finger his own hole. In fact he always supplied a latex glove since he was concerned about infection. Sometimes he brought along an assortment of dildos.

What about strap-ons?

You mean having the fem strap on a dildo and do him?

Exactly.

No way. He liked to play submissive, but he wasn't about to pull the plug.

What lure did submissive have for him?

Could have to do with his mom who died real young. Plus his stepdad was a ruthless white male who in all likelihoood buggered young Sean. What I'm trying to say is he came from a dysfunctional family that didn't know the meaning of love. Also he's hung so damn huge that maybe he got bored stuffing holes. Wanted to mix it up a little.

Well, he mixed it up a little by killing fems, didn't he?

True. But even murder can get old.

So let me get this right. He liked to do a fem doggy style while she was fingering his bunger with a latex glove?

You have a problem with that?

Just that it would take some dexterity.

With Sean's pole he had more leverage than the rest of us earthlings. You understand what I'm saying?

x

I mentioned Charles Manson to a Generation-X person and she was like: Who?

Manson? He ain't dead?

Far from it. He's doing life in Corcoran. Prison life agrees with him.

How's he look?

He looks great. Considering. That homemade swastika in the center of his forehead gives him a kind of dignity. Presence. He's pushing sixty-five. His teeth are shot. And that weird wildness that used to flash in his eyes when he was, like, trying to get into some fem's skull. Well, that look is fixed. Permanent. He's greyer of course. Though not that grey. And he still has most of his hair. Which he wears long in the old way. Greasy grey-black hair over his face and down his back. He looks like a prophet. Jeremiah or some shit.

Didn't his posse turn on him?

Don't believe everything you see on TV. He still has Squeaky Fromme. He still has Linda Kasabian. He still has Tex Watson.

I thought Watson became a lay preacher. I heard he got himself a large congregation down there in Texas. San Antone.

Subterfuge. He's doing devil's work under strict instructions from Charlie M.

Instructions conveyed. . . .

Telepathically. Actually Charlie has a tiny transmitter implanted in his swastika tat. Tex has a receiver under his scrotum. Which, probably you remember, was a pretty sizable number. Fact is, a lot of the fems actually preferred sex with Tex to sex with Charlie. But Charlie had those eyes.

What all is he instructing Tex to do?

Serial murder, mass murder, acid dreaming. . . . Charlie's still prophesying race war.

Helter Skelter?

Exactly.

What about the Million Man March?

Plays right into Manson's hands. Angry black brothers all in a row. Wouldn't that be some shit: Manson and his empire versus Farrakhan the ex-calypso singer?

Calypso singer reminds me of Geraldo. Didn't Manson and Geraldo go mano-a-mano?

Almost. It was during one of Geraldo's exposé deals. My money would have been on Manson. Even with his shot-to-shit choppers.

I've always meant to ask you this. How tall is Manson?

Harold Jaffe

Five-feet-four. Well, that's what he used to be. Now he's closer to five-one. Hard time shrinks a body.

xi

Dear Sean:

I'm an executive in the muscle industry with a real close nuclear family and grandkids. I've got everything I need—but excitement. You know how you keep playing back a great experience in your memory? A bunch of years ago in Vietnam as a Lance Corporal in the Marine Corps, I killed this girl. She was a hooker, but then I found out she was selling information to the Viet Cong. I strangled her while banging her, and I'm not exaggerating when I say that it was the most cock-throbbing moment of my life. The older I get, the more I miss it. If I could do it one more time, I'd be ready to meet my maker. Best of luck to you.

Dear Sean:

I dyed my hair red just for you and cut it real short the way you like. I have a firm athletic bod with great-looking plants with sensitive pink nipples, and if you suck them I'll cum. I have real long slim fingers that will fit perfect in a latex glove for me to do you while you're doing me doggy style. I just love blond, rough guys that are hung and uncut. After you do me you'll want to tattoo my name next to Jody's on your huge dick. Write to me soon at the PO address. Or you can fax me.

Dear Sean:
Hound-Dog's my name and bustin' serial bigs is my game.
You musta saw that layout on me in *GQ*. I'm the hottest
dick what is. And I'm sniffing out your raunchy butt, Sean.
You heard of the Night Stalker, right? Richard Ramirez? I
snatched his ass. He's jerking off on Death Row in Folsom.
Hey, he's more popular with the fems than you are. You
heard of Son of Sam? He's playing gin rummy in Attica.
When I copped him he promised to break out, cut my black
ass. He was a scumbag then, now he's a scumbag with
grey hair. Ah, my pager went off. An update on you,
motherfucker. Ima comin for yo ass and it gone be real
soon. Yours truly.

xii

A man and a woman
Are one.
A man and a woman and a serial killer
Are one.

xiii

Okay, I've brought you to multiple orgasms, now I'm
going to murder you.

*Wait a minute. If I knew you were going to murder
me I wouldn't have let you pick me up in the county fair.*

What about climaxing seven times—

Six.

Harold Jaffe

Okay, six. Isn't that worth dying for?

No. Twelve is worth dying for. Six is mild amputation.

Like what?

The small toe on my left foot. Or the first joint of the ring finger on my left hand. Or the anterior third of my left earlobe.

What's this with everything left? What about your right side?

Right side is eight climaxes, Sean. You only got me off six times.

Bullshit. I know what ecstatic moans are, and I counted seven. At least seven.

Those ecstatic moans and squeals were coming from you, lover. As I poked and pirouetted in your butt with four fingers of my gloved hand.

What do you mean: squeals? And there were no four fingers up me.

Yes there were. I was this close to burying my fist when you bucked and shot your load.

You're trying to put me down. Bust my chops. Sap my spirit. Just like all those other butch redheads. I'm going to snuff your ass.

No you ain't. (**Rips off his red-haired mask and Barbie-bodysuit to expose Hound-Dog, the serial killer buster.**)

What the fuck. You're an African-American male.

That's right, Sean. And don't tell me that's the first time you got down on all fours for an African-American male.

Well, like, I mean, shit. . . .

90

A little tongue-tied, aren't we? You see what I have in my fist?

A Desert Eagle .44 Mag semiautomatic. Cocked, ready to fire. What are you going to do?

I'm gone snatch yo ass, just like I said. Take you in live is what I prefer to do. But I could splatter you too if that's what you want. I'm Hound-Dog, P.I., and I go AC-DC. Hell, I go any which way the wind blows. Call it spineless role-shifting, if you like. That's what it takes to succeed on today's information superhighway.

xiv

After manacling Sean and displaying him off- and online like a freak, like they did that time with King Kong, they stuck him in a holding tank with an assortment of bad muthas. Big mistake. Sean slipped out of his leg irons, stripped naked, stood on his hands, stuck a guard's cap on his butt, and thus disguised swaggered out.

Just kidding. I'm not at liberty to convey just how he broke out or if he had any confederates and how high up they were. I'll just say he's out there in real time, humpin' his Harley, scouting for redheads, more videogenic than ever. Cheekbones. Designer stubble. Mickey Rourke voice. Those tats. That crooked freakin' grin. Not to mention what all's down below (you know what I'm talkin' 'bout).

Sean is free, white, twenty-three-years-old, and soaring.

If you have cropped red hair and a firm bod, you are advised to stay inside, online.

Open your mouth to laugh or yawn and he wheels and dives.

He's dew on the wing of the eagle.

And this fierce big bird don't just fly on Friday.

They call him Sean.

He will squat his firm high Chippendale flush on yo' face.

TWO

RODMAN

You're 6-8, 220. A tattooed, macho, kickass who's led the NBA in rebounding the last five years. Away from the hardwood, you make out like gangbusters. You even plucked Madonna's strings; she's still vibrating. You vroom around on a vintage Harley.

Yet you've shown an unusual sensitivity to issues like AIDS. You frequent gay bars and baths. You dye your hair weird colors. You pierce the most intimate parts of your body. You kiss dudes on the lips. You show up at your book-signing in drag, waving a feather boa.

There are contradictions here.

Who is the real Dennis Rodman?

Axin' me?

Yes.

Hey, I do what I do. It turn you on, cool. It don't, thas cool too.

Well, it's turning a lot of folks on. *People* magazine's annual survey of "America's 50 Most Fascinating People" ranked Dennis Rodman number 3.

That good news or bad?

Ain't no kind of news neither way.

Only President Clinton and First Lady Hillary were ranked ahead of you.

Thas cool.

You're not a registered Democrat?

What's that mean? Democrat?

If you don't respect political party designations, I guess you don't vote in elections.

Ain't never voted and ain't gone vote till they have the Motherfucker party. I see that, I vote Motherfucker.

Is your penis really pierced?

Yeah.

In how many places?

Twelve.

Tattooed too?

Yeah.

So you must have a heck of a lot of real estate down there.

Wanna see?

Maybe later. When we're offline.

(pause)

Your fling with Madonna has been well advertised. But some folks—including NBA basketball players, your teammates on the Chicago Bulls, for instance—are saying that's a coverup. You're really queer.

What's the question?

Why would NBA teammates say that that high-stepping kamikaze rebounder Dennis "The Worm" Rodman is queer?

Don't know and don't give a fuck 'bout what no NBA teammates be sayin'.

What *do* you give a fuck about? What rings Dennis Rodman's chimes?

Pain, funky music, oysters on the half-shell, speed, pain, a cool tattoo, violent contact, beautiful people naked.

Funky music? That include rap?

Yeah. Rap's cool.

What's your opinion of the OJ Simpson verdict?

Ain't got none.

Kato Kaelin?

Which one was that?

Blonde dude with the shaggy hair. Used to live with Nicole and was likely banging her. OJ got suspicious and put Kato up in one of his outhouses. Kato pretended to kiss OJ's butt, but then he pulled in big $$$ on the TV talk-show circuit saying contradictory things about OJ. A Saudi sheik allegedly offered him a million dollars to become the sheik's boy toy. Rumor is he bargained with the sheik, asking for two point five mil. Sheik said he would think about it.
    Kato Kaelin.
    Your impression?

OJ was fucking him.

Black activists have faulted you for not taking a stronger position on race issues.

You mean like black power?

Right.

I'm fuh black power. I'm fuh black and blue power.

You don't feel an obligation to be a role-model for black Americans? Especially kids? Inner-city kids?

Role model is a lot of hype. 'Cuz if there wasn't no inner cities wunt be no inner-city kids for Dennis Rodman to role model.

You surprised some folks when you gave big money to the family of that black man brutally murdered in Jasper, Texas by those racist yahoos. Chained him to their custom Ford pickup, scattered his head, body parts, dentures all over the back-country. Was it the black-white thing here that got your attention?

Was the damn murder. Plus the fact his people was poor. Plus me being from Texas.

(pause)

When you broke into the NBA with the Detroit Pistons you were a skinny dude with stick-out ears.
How did you grow all those muscles? Steroids?

No fuckin' way.

What about other substances? Crack, crystal, ice, Andro. . . .

I'm a clean machine. Thas it.

Rumor is Madonna hots for your pierced banana. You still on pretty good terms with her even after you refused her offer of marriage?

Fuck yeah. She knows Dennis Rodman ain't gone be marryin' nobody.

Don't mean to get too personal, but how was it doing Madonna? She pretty hot?

She ain't no acrobat. But she ain't no dead fish neither.

By the way, *People's* 50 most fascinating people listed Madonna at 31. Last year she was number 5.
Comment?

Axin' me?

Right. One year on top, next year a has-been. You concerned about your popularity fading?

Nope.

You're a great big dude by ordinary standards. 6-8, 220. But you're not that big by NBA standards. Especially for rebounders, guys like Hakeem, Shaq, Zo, the Admiral, Rik Smits. 7-foot muthas, 280, 300 pounds. How did you become a monster rebounder?

This *[pointing to his chest]*. **I have a big fuckin' heart. Plus I don't mind the pain. I like the pain.**

You strip off your jersey and toss it to a fan after every game. That means the Bulls have to come up with like a hundred Rodman jerseys a season. Has management said anything to you?

Nah. They don't like me doing it. 'Cept they love my rebounds and the money that come with winning, so they don't say nothing.

What about that fantasy you have of running down the basketball court naked?

Gone do it.

When?

When nobody expectin' it.

Likely be your last game in the NBA.

Maybe. I don't give a shit.

Have you ever reflected on your fame? The reasons for it. Is it the mixed messages that people cotton to? That tattooed and pierced one-eyed snake that Madonna's hankering to hump. But also the sensitive, animal-loving dude who maybe is a little bit queer.

What's the question?

Your fame. What accounts for it?

Won't take no shit from nobody. People like that.

Bad as you wanna be.

You read the book?

Bad As I Wanna Be? I surfed through some of the hard core parts. Making you some dollars, right?

Dollars ain't why I wrote it. I'm fuckin' rich already. I wrote it to answer questions people keep axin' about Dennis Rodman. Am I queer, am I this?

Okay. How would you answer that question: Are you queer?

You ain't been paying attention. I already answered it. These pigeon holes of yours don't mean squat to me.

You said you like pain. Ever bend for a dude? Get on all fours?

I squat. Lay on my back. Belly. I slam dunk. Bending ain't my thang. Too damn tall.

Whatever you are, you're a sexy dude to a whole lot of people. I guess you hump, what, every day? Twice a day?

Every day. More 'n that when I'm playing hoops is a lot. Sometime, though, shit come up and you gotta walk the walk. End up having sex a bunch, not getting no sleep, and the next day's a tough game on the road.

How do you play in those games where you didn't get any sleep the night before because you were up all night sexing?

Great. Some my best games.

Meanwhile the great Michael Jordan is in bed by 9. . . .

Sheat. Michael Jordan be gamblin' all night.

What kind of gambling?

Harold Jaffe

Depend where we're at. West Coast, he'll fly to Vegas. New York, he'll scoot out to Atlantic City. Else he'll shoot craps, play 5-card stud, flip quarters against the fuckin' wall, pee for distance. Anything, long as he can bet on it.

So I guess you sleep in the nude, right? Just you, your tats and piercings.

What?

You sleep in the nude? Naked?

Yeah.

Even in the Chicago winter?

Ain't sleeping in the fuckin' street.

You dream when you sleep?

Never. Sleep like a cat. Down and out for the count. But when it's morning I bounce right up, ready to fuck wit de world.

What about that time four or five years ago when you disappeared and were found a few days later in your Ford Ranger pickup in a parking lot with a 12-gauge and a Colt 45? Thinking of snuffing yourself?

Nah. I was just splattering rats in the headlights. I don't like rats. Know why?

Tell the worldwide internet audience.

Because they bite and suck poor people, babies, whatever. I grew up wit dem. They still around. Bloodsuckers.

Are you afraid of dying?

Hell no. It come fuh me, I go wit it. No big deal.

You don't like rats but you adore animals, large and small. Have you always been an animal lover?

Yeah.

You have an out-of-wedlock daughter, she—

Ain't gone talk 'bout that.

Fair enough.

(pause)

You've come a long way for an abandoned black kid kicked around foster homes. Hell, you were this close to being a black *homeless* kid. Alone on the cruel inner-city streets.

107

Harold Jaffe

But that was then. Now you're a 37-year-old musclehead jock freak pocked all over with tattoos and piercings. You're a fucking rebounding corporation. You humped Madonna. You tag-team with Hulk "Homo" Hogan for that wacky wrestling federation. You wear women's underwear—when you wear underwear. Shoot, you're in the process of redefining sexuality for the professional male athlete worldwide.

As for wealthy: you make enough money to bankroll Central Africa. You're number 3 in popularity only behind the President of the United States and his faithful spouse Hillary.

How does it feel being on top of the world, man?

Talkin' at me?

Absolutely.

What's the question?

Never mind. Who do you love most in all the world?

My cockatoos.

BOWLING

Story

In a case police called "beyond bizarre," the mother of a 14-year-old boy is accused of arranging a sexual relationship between her son and a 38-year-old woman.

Both women were arrested after the mother, feeling left out, reported the five-month affair to authorities, police said.

The boy's father, who allegedly knew what was going on, also was arrested.

All three adults were booked for investigation on a variety of child-sex charges.

Each could get up to 15 years in prison.

Meanwhile, the boy has been placed in protective custody.

Police are not releasing the adults' name to protect the boy's identity.

Discourse

*The mom reported the affair to the police because she felt left out? Does that mean the mom was getting it on with her son **and** the 38-year-old woman? How old was the mom?*

Yes, yes, 39.

Jack Benny's age. He played the violin.

He also possessed Rochester, his faithful, frog-voiced, Negro valet-clown.

The affair, or orgy, whatever you want to call it, had been going on for five months, right? How often would they get together?

Once or twice a week.

Where?

Usually at a motel off I-5.

Featuring hot tubs and triple-x-rated videos?

No. They didn't need those jump-starts.

Incest and child abuse were all the jump-starts they needed?

Bowling

Something like that.

[pause]

What about the dad?

Forty-three-years-old, six-feet-one with thinning brown hair and a salt and pepper goatee, high-bridged nose with flaring nostrils, prefers boxers to jockeys, likes large dogs, wears a size 11 shoe, roots for the Green Bay Packers, videotaped the action but didn't participate.

Admirable restraint. I gather the 14-year-old son is, er, precocious.

Slender, well-formed, dark-haired, with turquoise eyes like Liz Taylor in her prime. Plays tuba in his school orchestra.

Good lungs?

Excellent lungs.

What sort of family were they without the sex?

Typical American nuke fam with the white picket fence. Dad held a full-time job in junk bonds. Mom worked as a substitute 3rd grade teacher. Son got good grades and was popular with his classmates. They belonged to the Presbyterian Church.

Harold Jaffe

Presbyterian? Was this orgy about vanilla sex?

Are *ménages-à-trois* with your mom vanilla?

I mean was it just the customary ritual of orifice, penetration, ejaculation? Or was there any costuming, fetish play, watersports? . . .

Could be the mom was pissing the woman doing her son. Or the mom was pissing the son doing the woman. Or the son, disguised as Princess Di, was pissing both of them. Or the dad was pissing in his boxers while videotaping. Or the dog, wearing a Nixon mask, was raising its hind leg on the camcorder when the dad paused to take a leak.

What kind of dog?

Rottweiler.

Why did I have a feeling you'd say that? Did the Rot participate in the sex? Yes or no?

I just can't give you a firm answer.

[pause]

Tell me about the other woman.

Faux-blonde, pouty lower lip, twice divorced, born in

Bowling

Twenty-Nine Palms, that's in Southern California, won a trophy for line dancing in Anaheim, works off and on in retail, prefers tequila and diet tonic, is trisexual, trolls the Internet, never traveled outside the US, except for Tijuana, leases a mauve Mazda Miata, claims to have had a one-nighter with Bill Clinton when he was a Vietnam War evader, slam-bam-thank-you-ma'am, without much slam, according to her.

Trisexual, meaning. . . .

Male, female, indeterminate.

Indeterminate meaning. . . .

Your call.

Rottweiler?

If I said yes would you think any less of her?

On the contrary.

[pause]

How did the boy's mom and the other woman meet?

Bowling.

Harold Jaffe

Folks that bowl together ball together.

They bowled against each other. Each was the captain of the opposing team. They're both fierce competitors, if that tells you anything.

How did they work out the details of the orgy?

Three participants don't constitute an orgy.

I stand corrected.

The boy came to watch and videotape his mom bowl. The other woman saw him videotaping. She and the boy's mom already had a thing going. One thing led to another.

This other woman had children?

A daughter. She died while rollerblading. Nine-years-old. Run over by a metallic green Ford Ranger. The woman had a breakdown after that and was institutionalized. Broke up her second marriage. Took her almost two years to recover.

When she recovered she became a sexual animal?

Well, she decided to live her life.

Irrespective of the law and social mores?

She's on medication.

Prozac?

Zoloft and Trazodone.

I thought that stuff depressed the libido.

She takes Yohimbine to offset it.

[pause]

Was she abused as a child?

Who?

The other woman.

Sexual abuse?

Yes.

No.

[pause]

So the mom felt left out? Left out of what? The other woman's desire? Or her son's?

Both, I imagine. Primarily her son. Her son was her sun.

The sun used to be nourishing. Now it is poisonous.

So spend more time in front of your console. Or in bed if that part of you is alive and kicking.

What if the part is kicking but not alive? Or only partially alive?

Get it alive. By whatever means possible. Or murder the entity that murdered it.

I thought you were a pacifist.

That was the old me. Before the Millennium.

[pause]

Describe this woman who so loved her 14-year-old son sexually.

Lithe, graceful. Contralto-voiced. Majored in comp lit at Arizona State. That's in Tempe. Spent her junior year in Paris. Unwired. Reads Marguerite Duras in French. With a dictionary. Admires Jackie O, and like the mysterious billionairess, caviar and champagne are a weakness, when she can afford them. Bowling and sex are—were—her only exercise.

Bowling

She likes caviar and champagne but is unwired?

Does that make you uncomfortable?

On the contrary. She continued to make love with her husband?

More passionately than ever.

Fueled by fantasies of her son.

By whatever means necessary.

But the husband himself remained monogamous?

Depends how you classify sex in the head.

What kind of sex did he have in his head?

You name it.

Stuff with animals? The Rottweiler?

I said all I'm going to say about the Rottweiler.

[long pause]

There's one thing you haven't asked me.

What's that?

Whether the participants enjoyed the sex.

You mean. . . .

Whether the sex they had gave them pleasure.

Did it?

It was a rush. Bungee jumping, ethnicide, sky surfing, mountain biking—all that stuff gets old.

This didn't get old?

On the contrary.

And the boy?

You kiddin' me? Fuckin' loved it. Naturally he's p.o.'d his mom and dad and lover were arrested, but what's he supposed to do, right? Nobody's gonna listen to no jive 14-year-old.

CIRCLE JERK

Money Manager and Supermodel
at the Crowded Bistro

Please don't take this wrong. How long are your legs?

Sounds like sexual harassment to me. Inseam 32.

That's longer than mine. I'm a money manager. Do you mind my asking? What are you drinking?

Diet tequila.

You look like a supermodel. Excuse me. Are you?

What?

[Noisy bar. Rock music. Clanging pool balls. He shouts]

Excuse me. Are you a supermodel?

Yes.

I'm a money manager. I think I already said that. I'm a little nervous. Do you mind if I shout with you?

No problem. I have a few minutes. I'm waiting for somebody. He's late. He's always late.

I bet he has long legs. Does he?

Yes. And muscular.

What is he? I don't mean to be nosy. A model also?

Actor.

Oh.

In porno movies.

I didn't hear you.

In porno movies.

Oh.

[pause]

You yourself don't, uh, act, I guess, in, like . . . porno?

No, huh-uh.

[pause]

Can I get you another . . . diet tequila?

I'm still working on this one. So what's your deal?
You're a money manager with short legs. And you're look-
ing to get humped?

What's that? Oh. . . . Would you excuse me? I just
saw a friend of mine go into the Little Boy's Room.

Plumber and Mensa Member
at the Health Club

[On adjoining treadmills]

That's the high IQ thingy, right? How smart do you
actually have to be to be in. . . .

Mensa. Pretty damn. You're a plumber, right? I need
to snake out my drain.

Faulty drain, eh? I'm here to serve. Day, night, in
between.

You carry your snake on you?

Hey, does the inner-city female carry Mace? Does
the colostomy patient strap on his sewage pouch? I never
leave the condo without my snake.

Harold Jaffe

Where is it? In your Patagonia brand all-cotton jade sport shorts?

Right. You're sticking your lip out. You don't believe me?

No.

You're just used to those snakeless nerds from. . . .

Mensa. How many drains do you actually snake a week?

Depends on how many faulty drains there are.

How do you tell a faulty drain from a faultless drain?

No drain is faultless.

[pause]

You're really striding. Swinging those 5-pound dumb-bells in your fists. And I'm supposed to believe that snake is in your Patagonia sport shorts?

You sound doubtful.

The way you're chugging you'd think I'd see it. Swing and juke. Your snake is long, right?

Naturally. But it unfurls.

Unfurls? You mean it's short until it sees a sexy faulty drain?

Not short. Short is not a factor. The snake is long. When it unfurls it's longer than. . . .

Longer than what?

Than the rivers of blood that criss-cross this fucked-over century. How's that?

Money Manager and Serial Killer at the Public Urinal

Please don't take this wrong. But you piss like a horse.

I only go once a day. And this is it.

Once a day. Amazing. And you look like a guy that drinks a lot of beer.

I like my brew. I won't deny it. You're not doing all that bad. For a short dude.

I'm just about done. Few more shakes and that's it.

Shake, shake / zip 'em up. Sounds like you're just getting rolling. Pleased to meet you. I'm a money manager.

I'll shake your hand when I'm finished. Okay?

No problem. I can see that both of your hands and almost all of your fingers are engaged. I'll just lean against this funky wall. If it's okay with you. What did you say you did?

I'm a serial murderer. Sort of in between jobs.

Just about everybody I know is like that. Out of work or almost out of work. On the bubble. I hate that phrase. This darn recession. I guess I'm one of the lucky ones.

You, lucky? You look like a wuss with short legs. My guess is you're short all over. But you're good at managing money, right?

That's what I do, okay? And, yes, I'm good at it. Some time—if you're interested—I'll show you my commendations. Well, you're good at pissing. You haven't lost a beat. How many you kill?

How many? Twenty-two. Well, maybe twenty-three. One is still in the hospital. Intensive care.

Circle Jerk

Image Consultant and Serial Killer at the Stress Clinic

What triggers your panic reaction?

When I see a live body talking shit I want to shut it up. If I don't shut it up I get all stressed out.

Shut it up how?

Bust it. Splatter it. Hang it out to dry. How I take out a talking shit depends on my mood, right? Bottom line's the same. Dead doo. What's your thing?

When I see folks in public life that have absolutely no idea how to present themselves, first I get pissed, then I get stressed.

Give me a for instance.

Well, Hillary Clinton. The President's wife. She's too all over the joint. One day she's like super-fem-in-your-jock. The next day she comes on like Mother Teresa.

And your professional recommendation is. . . .

Super-fem. It's very hot. And she has the entitlements to support it, even with all the noise about rolling back affirmative action. Plus she's still young and good-looking enough to run with it.

129

[pause]

So you murder people? Mass or serial?

Strictly serial. Well, I might do two, even three, in one thump. Depends. And only if they get under my skin. Which seems to be happening more and more. I can't tell if it's folks getting shittier or me getting more thin-skinned. True story: I smell shit just about wherever I go.

Ha. Me, I smell shit, my pockets jingle. That's my job: turning shit that don't glitter into shit that glitters.

Uh-huh. At the same time shit that don't glitter stresses you out?

Exactly.

Televangelist and Pornographer at the Screening

I wear two diamond pinky rings and rail against sex. You wear two diamond pinky rings and stick it in our face.

Save your moralizing until you see the video, okay?

[After the video]

Well?

You're a foully fallen brother. It was even worse than I expected.

What did you expect?

More enticements. More knee work. Profound self-abasement. Far too many cum shots for my blood. For any Christian who's not just chewing cud. I thought you said Satan was doing a cameo.

We left Satan on the cutting room floor.

Tell me why, brother.

She lacked pizzazz. Her PR people promised lithe and rangy. What we got was short legs, chunky. And, naked, she showed fewer piercings than we were led to expect. As far as cum shots: they're my signature, Reverend. Plus that's what American viewers want to see. Let me modify that. Mature females like narrative. Little bitty stories with plots. But kids—I'm talking both genders—go for the explosive cum shot. So do their dads.

You claim that male *and* female chidren prefer the cum shot? Exploding splats? Jizz oozing down the face? Blowing scuzz bubbles?

Harold Jaffe

Polls have verified it. Don't you watch TV?

I watch myself, that's about it. Occasionally I'll look at a competitor. My schedule is far too busy for idle TV watching. Trawling through the world wide web.

You say you watch your competitors. I guess there's a shitload of 'em out there. Televangelists. It's a damn good living, right?

These are exceedingly trying times, brother. And pornographers like you add to the turbulence.

That reminds me. What did you think of the snuff scene?

You mean those naked actors in animal masks maiming and killing that young boy? Orgying in his blood?

That's the one.

I loved the killing and maiming parts. *Revelation* come alive. And an excellent depiction of our degraded culture. But the sex itself—poking, stroking, ramming, all that sweet spit, explosive cum shots, creamy jizz and blood cocktails—that left me cold.

Serial Killer and Mensa Member
at the Basketball Game

Slam dunk! Right in yo' face. Damn!

You sound like a Laker fan.

I'm an Indiana Pacers fan.

Look at that. Kobe stole it. All the way. Easy off the glass. He's a baby.

You alone?

I still don't like those droopy knee-length shorts they wear. What's that?

Clyde the Glide on the cross-over. Tasty move. It's rare to see a woman alone at a NBA basketball game.

What's a Pacer fan doing at a Laker-Rockets game?

It's Michael Jordan's influence. Those long droopy shorts. I was born in Indiana. I'm raising hell in LA now.

Indi-fucking-ana. I wish the Lakers had Reggie Miller.

Well, he played for UCLA. But he's real popular in

Hoosier country. You're alone, right? Your man or whatever didn't just go off to the concession stand?

Reggie's popular as long as the Pacers win. But how long will that last? You have large hands. I bet you can palm a basketball.

The Pacers' nucleus is young. They're only gonna get better. You're observant. I'm large all over. I can palm and—on a good night—I can slam-dunk.

There goes Barkley. Talk about large strong hands. He's great, but he holds the ball too long.

Hey, you know your hoops. What do you do when you're not at the game?

What's that?

Professionally?

I consult. Mostly I'm unemployed. Uh-oh, Shaq.

Coincidence. I consult too.

Shaq into the paint. Rockets gonna have to foul. Shaq's about to topple. There he goes. He's a huge strong guy, Shaq. But he can't keep his balance. You consult? What's your specialty?

His feet are too big. He's what? Seven-three? Murder. Serial murder. It's sexy. Everybody's into it. What about you? What's your deal?

Anything digital. Mathematics. Shaq is listed at 7-1, 315. He wears a 21 size sneaker, which isn't that large compared to other big dudes: Hakeem, Duncan, Patrick Ewing, even Rick Smits.

You're comparing apples with tangerines. Smits plays for Indiana. I know Smits. Smits ain't no Shaq. Do you like violent sex?

How vile is violent? Look at that Barkley. He just bulldozed Kobe the Kid. Ditch the coyness, okay? Toss your cards—face up—on the table. Let's see if you're the big bad motherfucker you think you are.

Pornographer and Triathlete
at the Healthfoods Boutique

I think I know you. . . .

You're blocking the aisle.

Sorry. From TV. ESPN 2, the Deuce. You're volleyball. . . .

Harold Jaffe

Triathlon.

Right. Right. You came in first. . . .

Fourth in a field of fifty-eight last week in Torrey Pines.

Fifty-eight females busting their chops. . . .

You've got a problem with that?

No. Not at all. It sorta turns me on. What's your best. . . .

Time?

No, event. Swimming, bicycling. . . .

Cycling is my strongest event. Then running. I'm working on the swimming.

Uh-huh. I remember watching you on the Deuce, cycling for the gold, butt high in the. . . .

My goal is: improve in all three, bring my swimming time down two-and-a-half minutes, come in first in Maui.

Big-time prize money?

Big enough.

Circle Jerk

When's Maui?

June. Gives me almost three months.

You work out. . . . .

Every day. Soon's I buy some astragalus, I'm heading to the beach.

Swim right in the ocean. . . .

Sure. Glad you recognized me. Gotta go.

Wait. That astragalus is a woman's herb. . . .

Not really. I've got to go.

Wait. Do you, like, ever go out with guys? I mean in between working out for these tri—

I already have a partner.

How would you like to be in movies? I'm a pornog—

Sorry.

So you're absolutely monogamous?

That's really none of your business.

[She pays for the astragalus at a counter and heads out the door]

One last question. What's your height, weight and body fat?

Five-eleven. One-forty-two. Three-point-eight-per-cent body fat.

HOUSE OF PAIN

Me? I'm one of those easterners who's never made peace with the California freeways. But the orgy was in the house of pain, and the house of pain was in Anaheim, a stone's throw from Disneyland. Since I lived and loved eighty-something miles south in San Diego, I had no choice but to ride the freeway.

With moist palms I maneuvered the Corolla onto I-5 north, juked and twisted into one of the center lanes, accelerated to 68 mph, slipped in one of my old Stones' tapes.

Let it Bleed, in case you're curious.

I squeezed my gens. Hard. Well, semi-hard, which isn't bad for a stressed-out easterner strapped into a fire-engine red Corolla rocketing north on I-5 destination Orange County.

"Stressed-out" is overstating it. I was feeling some freeway jitters, true, but I was also fantasizing, constructing, deconstructing, envisioning the scenario of my first orgy.

"First" might give you the wrong idea. I'd done two at a whack lots of times, and a couple times I'd done three, but it would be stretching to call any of those an orgy. So when I got that invite to the house of pain I simply could not refuse.

But that freakin' drive. Following the signs, switching lanes, decelerating at construction sites, viewing the bad faces of the other drivers. It was a test for any Buddhist.

Harold Jaffe

I'm referring to compassion, seeing the brutal-eyed drivers from the subject position, daring, even, to love them. I've been known to call myself a Buddhist, but I flunked that test.

Do Buddhists do orgies?

Simple explanation. I identified with the sensualist Buddhas and Bodhisattvas of the Tantric sects. I'm talking about some transcendental humpers.

By the time I got to the fashionable split-level stucco house of pain just south of Disneyland, it was later than I'd expected, and I was feeling edgy from the drive. Which had to have been a factor in what would happen.

It seemed like everyone else was already there and into it. Naked fooks, seven and eight in a mix.

Sex toys, strap-ons, sweaty flesh-in-leather smells. The resounding clang of chains. Tattoos, cuttings. Stylish amputees. Heavy metal easy listening on the central CD. The unsurpassable smell of hash.

I felt like a kid on the Internet.

I was naked and I was prime.

Two fooks, moist and muscular, were shuffling toward me. One, with a shaved head, studded latex collar and heavy ankle chains, had the sluttiest shuffle. The other displayed nasty open sores on the face, neck and chest, each sore with a gold or silver ring through it, each ring adorned with a charm or pendant.

As I raised an arm to cuff them, the one with the slutty shuffle stroked my gens.

Guess what? I spritzed.

Shot my wad. Sprang a leak. Dropped the bucket in the well. Whatever you want to call it. Same result. I done came too soon.

Which provoked an ironic smirk from the slutty fook who'd stroked my gens.

I tried to play it cool, which wasn't easy.

Sure, I was still a little bit nervous from the drive and from this being my first real orgy, but premature ejac is not my deal.

I know how to hold my cream.

But, yo, I was a young and muscular fook, so I was good for another shot, right? At least one.

Four or five minutes later, or maybe it was three or four minutes later, I was hard / thick / ready to mambo.

Gentlemen, start your engines.

I swaggered toward a mix of eight in multiform embrace, gleaming asses, silver silicon dildos, long pink moist tongues, latex body bags, pumpin' peters, that sweaty leather smell. . . .

A legless amp on metal crutches peeing through a majestic penis onto the pervy mix, swiveled his superb instrument on me and hosed my thighs and gens.

That's all it took. Splat. I sprayed my jizz a second time. Heavy dose too. The amp that was pissing me smirked, then swiveled back to the congregation.

What now? Dry off, get hard and try to hold my cream for a third go? Or put my tail between my legs and skulk onto the freeway?

Limp-dicked and pulsing with golden tears, I hung

around for a while, viewing the action.

Then I walked into the dressing area like young Sean Connery as James Bond, springy, on the balls of my feet.

Saving-face gesture.

I toweled off, dressed and split.

I-5 south to San Diego.

That was then.

After a month or so of working my abs another orgy reared its raunchy head. Why abs? To get that washboard tum, that sixpack look.

See, it ain't only your gens that's front and center at an orgy. You want to look hot and you want to look fit. Muscular defined abs can compensate for a host of deficiencies.

The orgy? It was the same venue: house of pain, Anaheim, Disneyland exit on I-5. Same time: 10:00 p.m.

This time I left half an hour earlier. After doing twenty minutes of Tantric meditation to take the edge off.

I possess, in case you've wondered, a seemingly endless reservoir of cream, as well as the springs to hose the ceiling and walls. As Michael Jordan used to say a lot: I'm blessed.

To make doubly sure, I refrained from having sex for five days before the orgy. Longest period of enforced abstinence I'd endured since the Marine Corps.

I was pointing to the big O in Disney country and didn't want anything to impede me from a personal best.

Right. I pulled my fire-engine red Corolla onto I-5

North, stuck in a Nine Inch Nails tape, maneuvered into one of the center lanes, and settled back.

This time I was among the earlier arrivals at the house of pain. Some of the other early orgiasts included four midgets, three glandular giants, two *au courant* shit handlers, probably half a dozen amputees, a gaggle of tattooed, pierced and cut fooks, and female triplets with ZZ Top beards.

I say female but actually they were indeterminate-gendered. As were nearly all of the other participants. Gender-fast males and females were a rarity in the circles I humped and kicked ass in.

Which was okay with me. I guess.

In any case, I didn't have a choice, did I?

I was stoked and I was confident.

But I was wearing a stainless steel cockring, snug about my gens, as a failsafe just in case there was any urge to tip my cream.

I ambled through the two large adjoining rooms pausing at this or that presentation. One featured a chartreuse-haired loon with what looked like an advanced case of leprosy: fingers, toes, the tip of the nose eroded. Bound to a replica electric chair, with a bone through what was left of the nose, the leprous loon was being fucked in four orifices with electrified dildos.

Correction: one of the dildos was an actual dick, I think, dotted with electrodes.

One of the dildo bearers was making hoarse Kung Fu noises with every thrust.

The sexy leper's name was Kim, with a shit-eating grin.

I slipped into the mix, sidling toward Kim.

Whoa. Someone snatched my ass and slid a gloved finger up me. Or maybe it was a slim dildo. Shot right up to my prostate and when I felt that final pressure, I spritzed. Cockring and all, I tipped my cream.

Separating my buns from whatever was between them, I spun around. But whoever poked me had blended with the mix. Nobody noticed my thick pool of curd, or cared.

But now I was limp-dicked.

I sauntered away from leprous Kim to another mix featuring a fook on a swing. S/he possessed a real beard, pasted-on Groucho mustache, miniature cock and functioning vagina. I know it functioned because it was being fucked by a slender fook with a pig mask and a back full of knife cuts. Meanwhile something else, small and dexterous, possibly a squirrel, was sucking the miniature cock. Moreover, the seat of the swing was ripped open exposing the bung which was being humped by a thickly-veined double-pronged dildo, while the other prong of the 18-incher was inserted deep into the brown eye of one of the ambiguous triplets in the ZZ Top beard.

This zany set-up made me spring up thick and hard.

Striding boldly into the mix, I snatched the left thigh of one of the prostrate midgets and scrutinized his tat. It took up the tiny fook's entire back, from neck to thigh, was continuous and exquisitely rendered: a vision of the

Flood, the water surging as in that popular Hokusai print, but in this version it was an apocalyptic tidal wave: buildings, people, animals violently flung out away from its force.

I was so impressed with the tat that I came close to tipping my cream, controlling the surge at the last second. Composure regained, I was about to launch into some monster sexing when—you won't believe this—the lights went out.

The blackout which would last for nearly three hours was not confined to Orange County. Evidently the Republicans, in San Diego for the Convention, liked it very bright and very air-conditioned, and the sudden excess use strained the system.

Why didn't the orgy continue under candlelight?

Because orgy fooks are into viewing / being viewed. Plus, several of the mixes depended on electrified sex toys, electrodes on the sexing bods.

Shock the Disney.

Bottom line: I'd gone to my second orgy in the house of pain, tipped my cream three times, and still hadn't got humped.

When the lights finally came on I torqued onto the freeway and home to San Diego.

People think that once they get their abs lean, hard and videogenic, they can just flash them and relax. Not so. There's no day off in the land of the washboard abs. Hence I was at it every day for about half an hour, sometimes forty-five minutes.

147

Someday science will supply all of us with washboard abs. Shoot, they've already done it with lab mice. All it takes is a single genetic alteration to turn up our natural metabolic furnaces so that we burn more fat. We'll be able to eat as much as we want and still have great abs.

How did I know all this?

I was a junior-level executive in the muscle industry. Which was stressful but financially rewarding. Plus, I got state-of-the-art fitness equipment at cost. As well as online access to the latest soundbites from the world of science.

Besides work and working my abs, I do (I mean: did) leisure sports. Squash, racquetball, corporate slowpitch softball, mountain biking, inline skating.

And when I found time and partners, I humped. But no orgies. Not even close.

In my mind, though, I replayed the house of pain deal many times. Had those lights not gone out, I would have been doing some transcendental humping.

Tip my cream?

Nah. That problem had been taken care of.

Then, nearly seven weeks after the blackout, I got another invite. Anaheim orgy, house of pain, Friday night, 10:00 p.m.

I-5 north. Center lane. 68 mph. Metallica hitting all cylinders in the cassette player.

Back in the house of pain and naked, I sauntered to a mix featuring a 17-year-old prodigy named Skag. He had two cocks: one about 8 inches and slender; the other 6 1/2 and thick. Each was capable of full erection and copious spewing. That's not all: below his asshole, in the area of the perineum, he possessed a species of vagina, with labia and clit but no uterus. The flesh-tube was elastic; it became moist with excitement, but was hollow. You could spritz in it to your heart's content.

Skag's blond hair was cut short and he wore a monocle. He was a devotee of Germany between the wars, Weimar with its proto-Nazis and bizarre cabarets. Skag had learned about Weimar on the Internet.

When Skag viewed me he said: "I love your abs."

"I love," I said, "your two dicks and faux puss."

He seemed to falter at the word "faux," but recovered and laughed a disarmingly high-pitched laugh.

I paused at another mix centered around a mongoose that told Polish jokes. If the jokes proved unfunny the congregation shocked the creature with electirifed probes. Cruelty to animals disgusts me. I passed that mix by.

Waddling toward me now was something pink, seminude, indeterminately sexed, and obscenely fat, with shaven head and protruding pierced nipples, each with a large ring and a heavy padlock hanging from it. The padlocks were connected by a thick iron bar covered with a fur or pelt.

You know Leopold von Sacher-Masoch's cult novel *Venus in Furs?*

Call this one Cyclops in Furs. Perfumed, too, sweet, intensely floral. Didn't help. I could easily smell the body's foul secretions.

S/he resembled the barefisted boxer called Butterbean, 400 pigbelly pink pounds of maniacal aggression.

Harold Jaffe

I tried to swerve but s/he trapped me against one of the Sony high-definition TV monitors and attempted to stroke my gens with fingers the size of pickled cucumbers. And smelling about the same way.

Employing my powerful abs, I thrust away from the horizontally challenged pervert, pushed open the bathroom door then slammed it shut. Butterbean would never fit through the narrow door.

Except the bathroom was in use. One of the transsexual glandular giants was squatting over the toilet, peeing like a monsoon, the massive shaggy head almost brushing the ceiling. The other human, on his knees, with a shaved head full of ringworm and a homemade Manson swastika between the eyes, had two hands in the toilet to catch the pee, rinsing his [?] brutish, rapt face with the golden goo. Sometimes slipping one fist under and into the giant's distended bung.

Funky smells here too, but still preferable to Butterbean. I looked through the keyhole: s/he was still massively there.

At which point the glandular giant said in a hoarse voice that broke: "Use the window."

"Talking to me?" I said.

"You," the giant said. "Climb through the window, then use your muscular, videogenic abs to climb down the drainpipe. It ain't that high."

"But I'm naked."

"Take a towel, dummy," the ringworm human said.

Taking a last look through the keyhole, all I saw were

Butterbean's pink folds, I couldn't tell whether front or back.

I snatched a towel, tied it around my waist, and moved to the window which was narrow and two stories up. Opening it, I crawled out. I took hold of the metal drainpipe and prepared to shimmy down to the astroturf. I could feel my abs working. But with one of my legs draped around the pipe, it gave way, sliding back from the house, and I fell hard on my back onto the astroturf.

Make a boring story short: I tore the arch off my left foot and compoundly fractured my lower spine. My foot subsequently got infected and was amputated just below the knee. After eight months of rehabilitation, I was pronounced a partial amputee and semi-invalid, and sent back to work. The muscle industry corp that I worked for said they would find me an "inspirational" post but that I would have to accept a 70% decrease in salary. I accepted. What choice did I have?

Some fourteen months after the accident I got another invite from the orgy fooks in the house of pain in Orange County. Guess what? I went. First I had my head shaved and tattooed with a frontal nude of Kevorkian, the death doctor.

No freeway this time, since I couldn't drive. I took the train and then taxied from Disneyland.

Believe it or not, it turned out to be the best orgy I'd ever gone to. I was an amp so that I was in a sense released from having to shoot my wad. Which I couldn't do anyway because of the accident. I didn't miss it. Probed and pissed, zapped with electric dildos, burned with molten wax—it was a whole other thing.

Coincidentally, I saw Butterbean, but someone had to identify *him*. The whole presentation had changed. S/he must have lost two hundred pounds, the pigbelly pink skin was deeply tanned and s/he wore a Fabio-style wig: long, platinum and raunchy. S/he also wore a skin-tight indigo latex jumpsuit with a bare midriff which displayed washboard abs. A nametag velcro'd to the rippling left thigh said: Isadora.

S/he—Isadora—recognized me, sauntered over to the mix that was doing me and said: "Hello there. Glad you made it back."

To be honest, I was of two minds: Buddhist and non-Buddhist. The Buddhist wanted to wave genially and say: No biggie. The non-Buddhist wanted to kill *his* ass with the snubnosed Smith & Wesson .38 I'd slipped into my jock.

What I did was remove the Smith with my left hand, take aim with both hands and squeeze off five rounds. Isadora toppled heavily onto *his* side, the outlandish Fabio wig knocked askew.

Snuffing Isadora that way raised the intensity level of my mix exponentially. I could feel it as they did me up, down, back and sideways. I even managed to cum, first time since the accident, spritzing Isadora's corpse with long-deferred heavy cream. Which I guess is what s/he'd wanted in the first place. When s/he was four hundred pounds and foul and a Butterbean lookalike.

COWBOY

Cowboy

So he's a legit cowboy? Stetson, chaps, lizard-skin boots, the whole shot?

You forgot his cellphone. Which, thanks to galloping technology, is getting smaller and smaller. His is about the size of a postage stamp.

I heard of one the size of a Viagra 50 mg tab. What's the cellphone for?

His investment team, attorneys, cosmetic people. He's a venture capitalist and has to keep in the zone.

Venture capitalist meaning. . . .

Spot / hover / seize.

[pause]

So he's married? Or does he juke around? Like Donald Trump or Ted Turner before Jane?

He's queer. Check that. He's a F2M, pre-op trans-sexual, who's sexually attracted to males.

Pre-op? His surgery was incomplete?

He never got the phalloplasty.

Which means what? That he lacks a dick?

Correct.

I guess that would put a crimp in his line dancing.

On the contrary.

[pause]

He's white, right?

Who?

The pre-op transsexual cowboy.

Why would you ask that?

When you said cowboy I thought of the traditional image: lean, tanned, virile Marine Corps vet smoking roll-your-owns, listening to Merle Haggard tapes in his custom Ford pickup, calling women pals darlin', standing at attention with his hand over his heart for the national anthem at monster truck—

Cowboy

Stop right there. 'Bout every cowboy I know is into the militia and freemen thing. They're not going to sing any national anthem. They hate the freaking feds.

That applies to this . . . personage? This pre-op transsexual venture capitalist?

Absolutely. Why wouldn't it?

For starters, I wouldn't expect white militia males to cotton to his brand of cowboy.

Interesting you say that. This image of the macho, gun-toting, big dog-loving, weak-brained, evangelical militia male rancher is persistent as hell. But it's wrong.

Who's keeping the image alive?

The media obviously. Plus Wall Street.

Why would they want to perpetuate that kind of image of the militia?

Surprised you ask. To make pizzazzy soundbites. Big-time dollars.

Watching disgruntled, evangelical, out-of-work ranchers hold a town meeting ain't all that pizzazzy.

Harold Jaffe

You don't think so?

Well, it beats watching paint dry. But not by much.

[pause]

We were talking about the transsexual cowboy venture capitalist. How did we get into this other stuff? Ask me more about the cowboy.

What's his name?

Christian name?

Your call.

Lamar.

Good name. Does he ride or is he rode?

You mean. . . .

Horses.

He rides. Sure he rides. He has a stable of quarter horses. He busts broncs. He loves the ro-**day**-o. That's how he says it.

Where's he from?

Cowboy

Piscataway, New Jersey.

And he got his sex change in. . . .

Beverly Hills.

Academic shit?

Bryn Mawr. He was a female then. MBA from Wharton.

Top-flight schooling. His surgery came after Wharton?

Correct.

Why didn't he go the whole nine? Do the phalloplasty?

Why? Because having a dick ain't what it used to be. These days you're better off without it.

Because of state-of-the-art strap-ons, you mean?

That and politics. And fierce fem vigilantes. You heard of them, right? They fast-skate in large posses, packing bowies. They spot a dick with an attitude, they go for the jewels.

And if he don't have any jewels these fierce posse fems are left with egg on their face.

Exactly.

Where does he live, Lamar?

Divides his time between Coeur d'Alene, Idaho and San Francisco.

He wears his cowboy deal in San Francisco?

Fuck yeah. He's six-feet-five, with long legs. You remember Jack Palance in *Shane*? Lean and shit-eating. That's how Lamar looks in his chaps and stetson in San Francisco.

Except Jack Palance didn't have to sit to piss.

You sure about that?

[pause]

Six-feet-five. I didn't picture Lamar that tall. Long, lean cowboy reminds me of young Duke Wayne. You remember how Duke Wayne walked?

Yeah I do. Combination shy and swagger. Sort of on the balls of his feet, boots pointing down.

Cowboy

You know who taught him that walk?

Jane Russell?

Dick Nixon.

What? When was this?

Early forties. Nixon, fresh out of Duke law, was conflicted between going to Hollywood and DC. In his heart of hearts he wanted to be a movie actor. Not a leading man because of his nose and jowls, but a cowboy character actor. Gabby Hayes was his idol. Well one day Gabby, who would do a bunch of pix with Duke Wayne, phoned Nixon and said: We have this big young dude here walks like a fag. I'm thinking maybe you can help him. He was talking about John Duke Wayne.

And Nixon helped him?

Hell, he turned his floundering career around.

Duke didn't need a phalloplasty.

Noo. Duke was hung okay. Nothing compared to Coop, of course. Gary Cooper. That's another story.

[pause]

So Lamar. He makes his venture capital in northern Idaho or San Francisco?

Both and neither. Lamar does his shit electronically. Sits naked in his personal sauna with his heat-resistant powerbook.

Sits naked in his sauna without his phalloplasty.

You don't need the big sausage to make the big money, partner. Not in these times.

You know, I can understand Frisco. But Coeur d'Alene? Isn't that where all those white supremacists are? Isn't that where Fuhrmann the racist cop in the OJ case retired to?

So? Just because Lamar hasn't had a phalloplasty don't mean he can't rock. I got news for you: racists ain't hung. Racists hate their freakin' bodies. That's one of the big reasons they're hot now.

What are some other reasons?

Economics. Ain't enough to go around. Klan, Nazis, Freemen, the religious Right. . . . Every damn posse is fighting for scratch.

You say "ain't enough." What about those eight figure

*salaries corporate execs pull in? What about the billion a
day it cost to finance the Gulf War?*

You asked me to give you reasons for racism's big
comeback, okay? Another reason is illegals. White folks
are up to here with colored pobres sneaking in, working
for shit wages, taking money out of white American pockets. Still another reason is Clinton. Having a Jew in the
White House. . . . You're looking at me funny. I guess you
didn't know Bubba was Jewish.

No.

Shit. There's a whole lot of Jews in Arkansas. Moved
west out of Miami when the Cubans came in. Have you
ever noticed the way Clinton walks? Flatfooted. Take a
close look at his muzzle. In bright light you can see the
surgical ridges of his nose job. Goes real nice with the
frizzy hair, which he colors of course.

[pause]

*So I guess those are the reasons that pissed white
racists are at the top of the charts. How does the venture
capitalist pre-op transsexual cowboy fit in?*

Lamar? Lamar netted 23 point 5 mil last year. Enough
said?

SEX FOR THE MILLENNIUM

On his knees on the Turkestan-style carpet he inserts the red-as-blood anal beads (Texas Instruments): one, two, three, four, five, six.

Withdraws them: plip, plip, plip. . . .

Inserts the magenta anal plug, medium width.

Probing, torquing.

I'm ready, he coos, on his knees, ass (Banana Republic) lubed and spread.

She enters wearing apricot patent leather calf-length stiletto heels (Netscape), C-cup breast enhancement by Dr. Pepper, and a Good Vibrations velcro thigh harness, in mocha.

She pulls the plug roughly from his ass, shoves it in his mouth, and fucks him with her eight-inch, uncut, silver silicon dildo, also from Good Vibes.

Her name is Domina.

Fucks him utterly, clear sailing, up there as far she can go.

Snuff sex on the VCR, shot in Brazil.

Naked actors in animal masks maiming and killing a nine-year-old street urchin.

Orgying in his blood.

Produced and marketed by Disney Plus.

On her back on the Mitsubishi kingsize "hospital" bed.

Naked, shaved, pierced.

(Soon to be pissed. But I'm getting ahead of myself.)

She wears a 24-karat gold clit ring (Nordstrom's Specialty Boutique).

Legs way spread.

He enters in his Lands' End metallic purple latex sado-suit, straddles her, whips out his dick (engorgement by Nike), pees.

His name is Shane.

Spray, loop, dribble.

Her legs, puss, tummy, tits, ears, eyes, mouth.

Golden teardrops (Aramco) everywhere.

While she's jacking off with her prosthetic fist (Intel).

Question: Was that real pee that came out of his Nike-engorged dick?

Real as opposed to. . . .

Unreal, cyber, you know.

"Real" is a category designed and executed by white males. Technology is not unreal. Nor is nature, as such, real.

Circumsized, circumspect.

He is nonetheless what he's engineered to be.

Noisomely nonwhite.

They: 16 aryans with armbands, documentation, sharp-toothed knives.

They ketch him and bind him.

Him don't scream.

Perform their ritual which consists of spreading their orifices (Qualcomm), spitting through their teeth, chanting certain buzz words.

Yank his drawers down to his knees then lynch him from an ironwood.

Faux naturally.

The cutoff blood shoots to his dick.

Fattest erection he'll ever get in his briefish life.

They don't blindfold him so he can see himself in the Sony.

Shoot him with their camcorders.

Watching him watch himself pray then spray his jizz.

They clap and grin and grope themselves.

But not each other (Microsoft).

She's a go-getter, Claire's her name.

Her game: climbing the institutional ladder, validating the countervailing system of: Women want power same as men. Which includes power over their bodies (Yahoo! Inc.).

Except in the flies (theatrical term) fuss & fume the witch-burners: pious, sentimental rabble-rousers.

They fuckin' hate bulldykes.

Pardon my French.

Love their nuclear family and fire, from Apocalypse to bbq.

Which naturally includes patriotic fireworks.

Back to Claire or Clark, whatever the freak it calls itself.

Harold Jaffe

S/he binds her breasts.

Farts like a male.

Dreams of flying (Hewlett Packard).

Which is what her molecules do when she is ignited, screaming, sailing into the collective void.

Whatever.

They burn her bush, sip her blood, mouse out of that file into FAMILY.

Was she really a witch? Was that real pain that generated her screams? Were those real Christian patriots? Natural rather than programmed, virtual, hyper, cyber, faux?

"Natural" is a category designed and executed by hegemonic white males. Forget that and it's your ass.

So she catches him from behind and does the stranglehold deal.

Sleeperhold actually.

Strips him, chains him to a California sycamore (Pentium).

Straps on her strap-on, enters him roughly from the back, humping hard up and down then circular, counter c[l]ockwise.

Prey comes to screaming.

She smashes him hard in the mouth with her brass knuckles.

Not brass, but a lightweight synthetic compound that mimics brass without the mess (Black & Decker).

170

Smashes him a second time.

Knocks out three teeth and two porcelain crowns.

Humps even harder, deeper, ripping his rectum.

Withdraws the bloody shitty 10-incher (Taco Bell), shoves it in his bloody mouth, gagging him.

Tough love.

Produces an official eight-inch USMC Nightstalker Bowie and stabs his eye while fucking his mouth.

Stabs his other eye, throat, still humping.

Gropes between his legs, severs his gens, then pulls her bloody dick out of his mouth and fucks his front where the gens used to be.

Produces a machete and severs his neck.

His dripping, bearded head (Apple) looks hot to trot on the busted cement, which is what she whispers to him, tenderly, humping his ragged gash.

Pulls out slowly, lets the body sack slide, then squats and pisses on where his gens used to be.

Produces a light-weight butcher's cleaver (Phillip Morris) and splits both legs at the thigh, both arms at the shoulder.

Hoisting the bloody left arm stump like a staff or scepter, she sticks the fist in her cunt, slides right in.

Then up her ass, slips right in.

With the prey's left dead fist in her ass, she severs the left arm above the wrist, gets up, cleans and packs her instruments, saunters away.

More like a waddle than a saunter, probably because of the dead fist in her ass.

She's worked up a hefty thirst.

Iced Vietnamese coffee: two hits of espresso in a third of a cup of condensed milk (fat-free from Starbucks) would hit the spot.

Did you say they were sis and bro?
I didn't say. But, yes, they were.
So I guess incest is no longer the last great frontier? Sexually speaking?
Shoot. That frontier's been crossed and double-crossed.
And death? She profanes his body then snuffs him? Butchers his body for her own sexual investment? What's that called?
"Snuff & Butch."

I'm a fem and I experience more pleasure in sex.

I'm a male and I experience more pleasure in sex.

I have a puss and breasts and am alive all over.

I have a cock, I pierce and probe, I gush.

I wear a strap-on which is reliably long and hard. When it massages my G spot, I gush.

My gush is milk.

My gush is cream.

I have muscular buns and a pulsing brown eye.

I have pear-shaped buns and a pulsing pink eye.

Let's appeal to an expert. Someone who's been both male and female.

Who do you have in mind?

What about Jax, Michael Jackson?

Nah. Hillary Clinton?
Nah. Dennis Rodman?
Nah. Madonna?
Nah. What about Warhol? Christian name: Andy.
He's outta here. Dead.
Only temporarily. He's been cryonically preserved.
Till when?
The year 2001. Technology permitting.

Has Warhol really been cryonically preserved?
Uh-huh. So was his mother.
Warhol's mother?
It was one of his conditions.
Name another of his conditions.
That he be awakened to a recording of Liza Minelli
singing "My Heart Belongs to Daddy."
That's a Cole Porter tune, right?
No. Paul McCartney.

War in the Red Sea.
Those wogs insulted our flag (Pfizer).
Not once but repeatedly.
Now there's heck to pay.
We'll do what we can to prevent civilian casualties.
Children and so forth.
Except those gooks start real young.
Adolescents with identical black mustaches (Chevron).
Throwing rocks and there are billions of rocks in their
desert lifestyle.

Harold Jaffe

Along with razor-sharp scimitars, invaginated females, mega-strong coffee and hashish (John Deere), which they mix with tobacco and inhale through those outlandish long pipes.

Between bending to Allah and cruelly punishing transgressors, they're big spenders, but Jockey and Fruit of the Loom would bat zero in their fancy desert because the sheiks don't wear any drawers beneath those floor-length kaftans.

They blame the heat but our sources say they have underage white slave boys under their kaftans.

A-suckin' and a-tuggin'.

Now we're going to kick their ***** with our surgical strikes, smart bombs, infinite technology.

If they start messing around with chemical warfare, nerve gas and so on, we'll go the nuclear route and broil the freaks (Saks Fifth Avenue).

Our promise to you is that this will be our most viewer-friendly war to date.

Stay up-to-the-minute by tuning to our web site. www.blud&sand.gov

The title of this thing is Sex for the Millennium, but some of the foregoing sequences aren't sex per se, right?
Right.
*But I guess they are **sexualizable**. Depending on the viewer-consumer's net income, hi-tech savvy and devotion to the program, right?*
Right.